Artificial Stars

Carmen White

Sky Circle Publishing

Artificial Stars

Author: Carmen White

ISBN: 978-1-956229-07-3 (print)

ISBN: 978-1-956229-08-0 (Ebook)

Publisher: Sky Circle Publishing

To my family, with love.

Thank you for all the hugs and support.

Contents

Chapter 1

E laine lay on her back, half underneath the kitchen console. The chinjk flickered weakly around her like tiny shards of crystalline glass, but the gaps and incorrect pieces of the puzzle stood out like an ugly wound. Luckily, when it came to computers, she was the expert, their surgeon, their artist. Assuming, of course, that the owner wouldn't keep breaking it time and time again.

Above her, Mr. Josefp paced the floor of his apartment in a shuffle. He was an elderly man, well over a hundred and fifty. A retired software developer with too much free time on his hands. He *should* have had some understanding and respect to *not* mess with this sort of thing. But no.

As she carefully fixed his computer for the umpteenth time, pulling new chinjk pieces from her work tote and laying them carefully inside the console to complete the broken pattern, she couldn't help feeling annoyed, despite the satisfying glow that appeared whenever she got a piece placed correctly. "Are you going to tell me what the heck you were trying to do this time?" she asked.

"I need a second system," Mr. Josefp said. "And I want them both to run faster."

"Why do you need a second system?"

"In case there's a wipe," he said.

"A wipe?" she muttered. *What the crap is that supposed to mean?* She eased her short fingernails into the next panel and carefully peeled the pure-foam back to uncover the interior. She frowned at the dirty work it revealed. Had he actually tried to *glue* the chinjk in? Who in their right mind would do that? She set her chinjk box aside so it wouldn't spill and scooted out from under the mess. His apartment had a rustic feel to it: blankets, pillows, real bookshelves with real physical books, and a soft dim lighting to everything. Of course, the dim lighting was more due to the Arkinee-style glow sticks he was using for light - since he destroyed his entire house system trying to 'make it run faster'.

"You don't know what the Wipe is?" He threw his hands in the air. "Ugh. Of course you don't. No one remembers it!"

Elaine glared in annoyance. "Mr. Josefp." She pulled her chinjk box out from under the console and took a thin scale out for him to see. "What color is this?" she demanded.

"Pinkish." Mr. Josefp said. He paced back and forth by his kitchen counter like an encaged storm. "Reminds me of a fish scale."

"It *is* a scale: an Engern scale. And that's the way *you* see it," she said. "That's the way it looks to most of us humans. The Kreet see it as grays and silvers, the Arkinee say it's white, but in general they all think it looks pretty boring. *Except* to an agent. To us agents they look different: blues, teals, greens, purples, gold. And each one has a certain shape and texture that only agents can see and feel."

He frowned at her.

She sighed and clicked the piece into the damaged holograph panel on his countertop. "My point is, maybe let the professional handle things when you need your hardware changed?" She ducked back under the consol.

"I'm not stupid," she added, in case he was still hung up on the whole 'wipe' or whatever he was upset about.

"I didn't say you were stupid," he said. She could hear the tiredness in his voice, feel him move past her as he set his arms on the other side of the counter. "In my day we had real material," he muttered unhappily. "Not scales from some weird space monster no one actually knows anything about."

"Yeah, but wires and electronic circuits can't power every form of tech in the *entire* universe." She snapped another piece of chinjk in place like a sharp punctation to her sentence. "You're welcome, by the way. Can you imagine how vulnerable old computers probably were? Or more important stuff, like your heart implant?"

"I'm well aware, Elaine. Thank you," the man said, through gritted teeth.

He wasn't truly angry. She knew that because angry people made her skin crawl in warning, and she never felt that with him. He was upset, though, and she couldn't stand that sad, weary tone to his voice. She let out a slow breath. "What's a wipe?" She asked, trying to sound more interested than she felt. She tapped her wrist to activate her Sp-ACE's flashlight setting while she looked over a particularly nasty spot of chinjk.

"Before first contact on my planet, there was a Wipe. It took out all our tech: electronic, digital - anything above basic electricity. It will happen again."

"You guys ran into the Kreet first, right?" she asked.

"Yes."

"Are you suggesting they purposefully sabotaged you?" She frowned. She generally tried to stay away from discussions of both race and politics, and especially away from where those two subjects intersected. But, like most old people, race and politics was about all Mr. Josefp had left to talk about.

"I'm not saying that," he said. "I'm saying someone, or *something* destroyed it. Every time someone comes close to discovering artificial intelligence, there's a Wipe."

Elaine frowned. " You mean AI? Like those books you've been lending me?" Every time she'd come to fix something, he'd stick an old fashioned - as in actual physical paper – book in her hand and insist she read it. It was some old fictional stuff about housing programs that could think for themselves, apart from programmers, and weird stuff like that. She'd scanned through them. But she preferred comedy and romance to speculative, especially the creepy speculative. He said authors of old wrote such things to predict the future, or for escapism, but Elaine didn't care much about the future. She was quite happy with her life as it was now.

She'd grown up on a planet where the modern technology the station enjoyed had been strictly banned. Not the happiest life for an Agent, growing up with a gift. She had been bluntly ignored at the best and severely disciplined for it at the worst. But she didn't have to worry about it now. Besides, even if there was a 'wipe' on various tech, chinjk could power anything. This station alone, spinning slowly around the Engern Sea powered the planets within its system with tech that rarely wore out and was computable no matter the planets history and technological advances. She didn't need to think about it, worry about it, or let her mind go back to a childhood she feared and hated. She shook the memories out of her head.

"Yes, like the books."

"They're fictional books, Mr. Josefp. Old, weird ones at that." She scooted out from under the console. "Let's see if that fixed it. Turn it on." Mr. Josefp swiped his wrist across the diamond shaped sensor plate and his home program popped up in holograph, glowing a soft greenish blue. The lights in the kitchen and living area came on soon after and the house settings tested the lights, water, and environment before adjusted to its default settings.

"You're an angel."

Elaine chuckled. "A what?"

"An angel: a messenger, guardian of lore. They either come for vengeance or to assist."

"Oh. Well, that's me alright, vengeful assist-er." Elaine sighed. "Look, I could technically start a second system if you really want it, but I don't think I'm going to be able to just write 'guy wanted second computer' on my files without the higherups raising eyebrows."

"I'll pay for everything myself. I already have most of the parts."

Wow. He's serious. "Let's see it, then," Elaine said. She would still have to make her own trip to a shop to get everything. Luckily, this was the last call of the day - and who could say no to an extra and non-government-controlled gig?

"I'll get them," Mr. Josefp said. "Would you like some coffee while we talk out plans?"

"Sure, thanks. That sounds really nice actually."

"I bought some cookies yesterday. We can have those, too," he said.

It took several hours and two trips to the shop to track down parts, but Elaine felt pleased with her work by the time she was finished. It felt good, starting a project from scratch. She hadn't done that since her lessons at the college. Most of the time she just did repairs. And now that Mr. Josefp had his all-important second system, maybe he'd get to work on whatever program he was working on and stop messing around with the hardware.

He handed her the box of cookies they hadn't quite finished. "Take these home with you. I'm sorry I kept you up so late."

"No problem. It was actually really fun." When she reached for them, he put his hand on top of hers, expression becoming strained.

"Are you alright?" Elaine asked.

"Thank... Thank you. Yes, I'm fine just... thank you. For everything you do."

"Yeah... um. Like I said, it was fun. Don't forget to register your new system when you get the software running. It'll just walk you through it. Okay? Id' rather not get fired."

"Of course," he replied. "Of course. You have a nice night, Elaine."

She waved to him again as she walked past his little terrarium of earth flowers and down his apartment steps to the street. She glanced back once to make sure he'd gotten back inside his home okay, then shook her head and headed home herself.

This sector of the station had been set to night ambiance. Not that 'night' meant much here. The station circled a cosmic ocean, not a star. And an active nightlife - or someone else's day - was, at most, a 30-minute shuttle ride away. Still, it was a nice thought. Beautiful in its own way. From street speakers she could hear the occasional sounds of strange crickets or nightbirds chirping. Artificial stars pulsed upon the dark navy ceiling, several miles above her head. The pattern of light was long and complicated, but she recognized it without looking it up on her Sp-ACE. Tonight's star charts were set to match the Arkinee homeworld, North hemisphere. That should make her neighbors happy.

Since her own apartment wasn't far, she decided to walk instead of taking a shuttle. Soon, her head felt clearer and her shoulders less sore. Today was good, she decided; a lot of work, a little unexpected, but just the right amount of both of those. When she turned onto her home street, she was not surprised to see her neighbors out and about visiting and enjoying their night sky. The apartments here were side by side. Glowing magnets decorated the front of buildings and the streets in alien symbols and jokes that no matter how much they tried to explain to her, she just couldn't quite get. The Arkinee were nocturnal by nature, which was why Elaine had been assigned her more human-size apartment right on the edge of the sector. No one was going to actually *pay* for it, not with such noisy neighbors on the other side of the wall. Government officials decided that if no one was going to take the too-close human apartment, they might as well make an employee live there.

Due to their biochemistry, the Arkinee were vulnerable to oxygen, carbon dioxide, and high moisture. So, when they were away from their home planets, as they were now, they zoomed around places in egg-shaped pods, tightly sealed to keep them safe. She repaired several every year and did regular chinjk maintenance to keep them properly powered. Each pod made an odd whining sound when it was powered on, similar to that of a crying child. Once she had gotten used to the peculiar noises though, Elaine found she didn't mind them. In fact, she'd found that, instead of irritating, her neighbors where some of the kindest, most empathetic people she'd ever met.

One of them, named Zultra, zoomed up to her now, hovering her pod what was considered a polite distance away until Elaine stopped, accepting the greeting.

"Good evening, Zultra."

"Good morning, Elaine," the alien replied. She was small, only about five and a half inches tall, with a willowy body, and, like the rest of her species, waking now for their own, much daker version of 'daytime'. Her voice emitted clearly and loudly from the external speakers on her pod. "Also, I want to be called 'Ultra Zultra' now. Do you approve it? I have been thinking of the word, and I like it very much."

"I like it." Elaine said, which was really the only appropriate answer, so it was a good thing she really *did* like it. The Arkinee had weird naming conventions that Elaine had trouble grasping, but it had something to do with everyone else in the community agreeing to it or something. Elaine was both nervous and honored by Zultra—Ultra Zultra—wanting to include her in the decision. The tiny alien pulsed a neon glow briefly, a neon yellow glow in happiness, Ultra Zultra shook it away and asked Elaine how her day had gone.

"Did an entire overhaul on a system," Elaine replied. "It was fun."

"I'm glad you had fun! I got a message from my uncle today. You will never guess what he did."

"What did he do?"

"Discover a planet."

That sure made Mr. Josefp's system fiasco seem rather wimpy by comparison. "Really?"

"Really! They don't know if there's life on it yet, but they're going to find out."

"That's... really cool."

Ultra Zultra nodded happily. "Are you tired?"

"Uh?" Elaine shook her head, trying to rewire the sudden change in conversation that her friends were so prone to. "A little."

"I won't keep you long then. I just wanted you to hear my new name! I was a bit worried you were so late. I'm glad it was for a good reason and a fun thing. If you can't sleep and get lonely, you can visit. But I do hope you sleep well."

"Thank you, Ultra Zultra."

The alien grinned happily. "Oh, it *does* sound like a good name, doesn't it? I love it so much. Goodnight, Elaine!" She zoomed away;

the squeal of her pod was loud until she slowed upon finding someone else to talk to and it fell to a lower whining squeak.

Elaine smiled, shaking her head to herself. They were a bit on the nosy neighbor side, but they were just so honest about it! She walked to her own apartment and swiped her wrist across the door lock. The door opened and the dim lights flickered on. Similar to Mr. Josefp's apartment, the kitchen and living room were side by side, small, with a few fake windows to give it the sense of space, even though there was none. Her bedroom and bathroom were in the back, and really, that was all there was to it. She'd found ways to make some personal touches though, starting with the glowing chinjk light covering the room in delicate circuitry shapes. She'd pulled the exacta-foam off when she'd first moved in. It was prettier this way. It pulsed pleasantly in a rainbow glow around the room, connecting to the consoles on the desk, kitchen counter, television arrangement, and running like a streamlet of gems down the short hall to the bedroom and bath. The design was unique to the apartment and the individual agents who had worked on it when the apartment had been built. Elaine set her work box and cookies on the kitchen counter. The countertop read the cookies and added them to her pantry list, though she didn't see much of a point. She'd probably eat the rest tonight anyways.

After a warm shower, and the rest of the cookies, Elaine lay down in her bed and brought up a movie to watch. It was a Kreet romantic comedy, so some of the smut was a little weird, but the plot and characters were fun enough. After four episodes she began to feel both relaxed and tried enough to sleep. The hum of her apartment and the night-life noises outside began to have a white noise she could synch her thoughts too.

Then suddenly, it all just stopped.

Silence.

The holographic screen went off, and even the glow of her chinjk faded into blackness. She sat up with a start, disoriented and dizzy. It was so dark she couldn't tell for certain which direction she was facing, or what was up, down, or sideways. "What the...?" She tapped her wrist for light, but her Sp-ACE wasn't working either. No coms, no light, no anything. She stumbled to her feet, tripping over the pile of laundry she still hadn't washed. She felt her way to the front door, but it wouldn't open. "Come on, open..." Nothing was responding.

More slowly than it had vanished, the lights came back on. The chinjk on her wall warmed up to its pastel rainbow glow. Her movie came back on, glitching once, then playing the famous in-law scene as if nothing had happened. "Pause my show," Elaine commanded, not so much for worry of missing the drama, but just to make sure the housing software was back online.

The show paused obediently, and the door finally opened for her. Rushing out onto the street in relief, Elaine took a deep breath. *That was weird.* She took another breath to calm herself. Maybe her housing chinjk was damaged, though she couldn't think of anything that would have wiped out the whole system. What on earth could have caused...?

It was still so... quiet.

Elaine turned slowly, watching as colored windows pulsed gently to life among the sputtering glow-art. The streetlights came back on one by one and that's when she saw all the crashed pods. "Zultra?" She ran toward them. The Arkinee changed the color of their pods as often as they changed their names, so she wasn't sure whose was whose; she just started calling names. "Arisa? Avirii Friend? Dark Danikim?" She turned over a toppled pod. The tiny body, bloated and discolored, rolled lifelessly inside the glass shell. Elaine choked and stumbled back, putting a hand to her mouth. Shaking, she turned over the next one. They were all dead.

Chapter 2

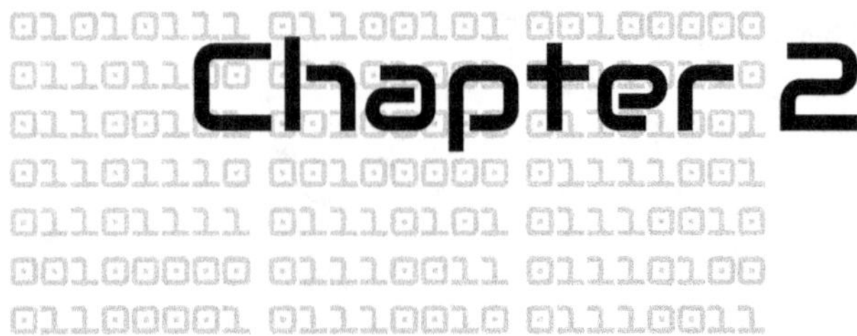

I **'m sorry. There is a problem with our system. Please remain calm. We are working to resolve it quickly.** Her Sp-ACE kept repeating itself no matter who she called.

Holographs atop buildings and on street signs said the same thing:

I'm sorry. There is a problem with our system. Please remain calm. We are working to resolve it quickly.

Elaine ran down the streets as fast as she could. She stopped every time she saw a tipped-over pod, but found that not a single one of her neighbors had survived. She had called the police, she had called the hospitals, but she kept getting the same message.

"Please state your emergency and help will arrive as soon as possible."

"Something happened," she said. "There was a power outage. It just... Everything went off. The Arkinee are dead! I need help. I can't... I don't know how to..."

How to *what* exactly?

Bring people back from the dead?

Even if help came, it was too late. She stopped in the middle of the street, surrounded by toppled pods and terrible silence. She clenched her trembling hands.

Somewhere through her own breath, too loud in her ears, she heard people yelling and screaming throughout the station. She ran towards that proof of life as fast as she could, away from the dead silence. In the next sector, she found people. Mostly Kreet, running through the streets in dazed confusion. They called out desperately to family members and friends.

Several shuttle cabs had crashed into the side rails along the deep, wide shuttle ways. Elaine held her breath as she neared the broken highway railings. If the flying shuttlecraft had lost power, not everyone would have been able to make a landing. On an airway that was nearly as deep as the station itself, that meant... She found herself staring down into the pit, the wreckage at the bottom so far away she couldn't actually see it. But the emptiness of what had always been a constantly busy road was enough to confirm the worst. Those around her swore and cried. They made frantic calls much like her own, telling impartial software what had happened, trying to explain to a machine that loved ones were gone. Forever.

"Help!" The voice belonged to a human woman who was struggling to climb out of a crashed shuttle, one of the 'lucky' ones that had toppled sideways against the railing. The woman was trying to climb out the side door, now facing up, and the vehicle tilted dangerously under her weight.

"Hold still!" Elaine ran up to the woman. She wasn't the only one answering a cry for help, there were so many of them through the station now. Her head buzzed as her translator tried to pick up everyone, turning the sound around her into an echo of white noise punctuated by too-loud voices. She braced her foot against the base of the shuttle way rails and reached over toward the shuttle. "Is there anyone else inside?"

The woman shook her head.

"Take my hand." They grabbed each other's wrists tightly. Elaine leaned back as the shuttle started shifting. "I've got you. I've got you!"

As the woman steadied her feet for the jump, the shuttle rocked and started sliding into the abyss. "Jump!" Elaine shouted, jerking hard. The woman tumbled toward her, falling onto the hard street as the cab vanished over the lip of the highway.

"Are you okay?"

The woman nodded. "I-I'm fine. Thank you." She stood slowly. "What happened?

"I don't know," said Elaine. "The power went out."

The woman pressed her palm to her temple and blinked rapidly. Elaine noticed a cybernetic flash to her eyes, an almost pinkish light. Maybe to others, the artificial eye matched the woman's natural one, but to Elaine, the intricate chinjk work glowed, pulsing faintly before fizzling out. "You need a hospital."

"I'm fine. My vision implant went out when the shuttle did. But I can handle it, I'm a nurse. We need to get everyone- "

Elaine spun and ran down the street.

"Where are you going?" the nurse cried out behind her.

"My friend has a heart condition!"

"Hold on! Wait for me!"

He'd warned her about the Wipe. He'd stood there in his kitchen and told her exactly what would happen.

"Before first contact on my planet, there was a Wipe. It took out all our tech, electronic, digital, anything above basic electricity. It will happen again.... Any time someone comes close to discovering Artificial Intelligence."

The pleasant nighttime walk that she had enjoyed only hours before turned into a frantic run, taking every half-formed thought, every last breath she had, as she came to the house. "Mr. Josefp?" The door swished open for her. "Mr. Josefp?"

His body lay in a crumpled heap on the kitchen floor. She should help, she should do something. But all she could manage was to dig her fingernails around the edge of the countertop and come no closer, because if she didn't hold onto *something* she might fall into some dark hole. A hole that, in her head, surrounded those that were dead, and it wanted to take her too.

A weird rhythmic sound grew louder and louder, like a too-quick heartbeat, but it was only footsteps. The woman Elaine had rescued appeared in the doorway briefly, before hurrying to the body. She scanned for signs of life with her Sp-ACE, and finding nothing, pressed her fingertips to Mr. Josefp's wrist.

"He had an artificial heart," Elaine whispered.

"I'm so sorry," the nurse said.

What was anyone supposed to say to that? Elaine looked away as the nurse tried to contact more medical teams, some kind of help. "I don't understand..." Her friends. The power. It had only been off a moment. *What if power went out in the Sea too?* Her stomach tightened. She didn't know she could feel any sicker. "I-I have to check on something." She ran out the door, past the terrarium, and toward the highway.

What if the Engern are dead too? Elaine hurried down the street until she found a shuttle that wasn't crashed. She slid into the seat and passed her wrist over the console chip, hoping her emergency ID would be active by now. It denied her the first time but worked on the second swipe. "Sector 10, inner docking 12," she told the shuttle program.

As the shuttle swept into the chasm-like highway, she felt her stomach do a somersault. *What if it all goes out again?* What had used to be an ever-moving highway was empty now, save for the emergency vehicles that sometimes appeared on her level, only to swoop downward, checking to find survivors amid the wreckage below.

She couldn't imagine it happening again, but she also realized how foolish that was. She had no evidence that she was safe here. For all she knew, this disaster was galaxy wide, or other power stations had also been hit. If the Engern, were dead, the station would lose everything; every job here, all the restaurants, entertainment, museums, and colleges were only here because this station was the power source for the worlds around it. *Please be alive, please be alive.*

When she finally reached her destination in the inner sectors, where houses were larger, and shops more refined, she jumped out of her shuttle and ran for the viewing windows. Along the streets, even the important and well-to-do were suffering, crying in fear and mourning lost friends. She had a fuzzy sort of awareness about it all. Her vision seemed to darken around the edges, and she could only focus on what was directly in front of her.

Her heart pounded as she stopped in front of a wide, five-story high window. Here on the inner side of the station, all windows looked in at the Engern Sea, a beautiful ocean of light. Swimming in that vast sea of light were the Engern. Alive. Their precious power-giving scales shimmered in various shapes and patterns. Some of the creatures were as small as her hand, others larger than shuttles. They swam in the energy around them like it was water, giant tails carrying plump, bulbus bodies driven by arrow-sharp heads. To her eyes it was a calming dance of pinks, blues, and light greens, an ocean of energy that pulsed and moved with life.

She pressed her hands to the window, then laid her forehead against it, breathing out slowly, and realizing only now how light-headed she felt. *At least they're okay.*

She found herself truly exhausted, shaking. She sank to the floor and pressed her back against the window like it might shield the Engern somehow, before putting her head in her hands. *I need to do something.*

"Do you need help?" a voice asked.

Elaine jerked her head up and stared at the stranger. They were tall, with teal skin and near-white eyes. She registered this, and recognized it as unusual, even for people on the station. She didn't recognize the species, but she did recognize the uniform. She stood up quickly.

"I'm fine," she blurted. She hadn't seen an Investigator since school. Investigators and agents were trained on the same campus, but at the warning of her roommates, she'd never really interacted with them. Death Detectives, they were sometimes called. People who, like her, had abilities, strangely natural and yet ridiculously rare.

"G-go haunt someone else," she stuttered.

The Detective cocked their head to the side, perhaps waiting for their translator to catch up. "Haunt?"

Elaine flushed, bracing herself against the window for support. Today was too hard. Everything. Too hard to handle. She found herself wanting to burst into tears, but that only seemed to make the alien more concerned.

Elaine worried the Investigator might read her behavior as something suspicious or criminal. The thought that they could rip all her memories out of her very soul was terrifying. "Don't touch me."

"I'm not," the Investigator said. Mirror-like eyes seemed creepily appropriate for someone with such an ability. It was unsettling. The rest of what they said didn't translate, and she wished they would just walk away.

Finally, the alien complied. Raising two fingers of a six fingered hand in some sort of sign and backing off.

She took a shaky breath and wiped her eyes on her sleeves. *Pull yourself together.* She looked back out toward the Engern. *They're okay. I'm okay.* Now she just needed to do her part. Needed to help, to fix everything. She looked at the Engern one last time. "It's going to be okay," she promised.

She opened a display on her Sp-ACE. It was updating every few minutes with new notifications and her normally-assigned work area had been canceled, allowing her easy access to the entire station as needed.

The topmost notification requested that all agents even lightly trained in Medical chinjk report to the nearest hospital. That kind of work was a little too unsettling for her, so she'd never gotten medical training.

She pressed the filter to her level and skill set and tapped the biome needs selection. Her extended range revealed several emergency spots that needed repair and she responded to a couple. She'd stop at the nearest gathering center for more chinjk, since she was so near the Sea right now. There would be a growing risk of black-market pirates stealing it, even with the emergency laws in place.

She could do this. The list of instructions, of actions she could take, was comforting. It gave her focus. She'd do everything she possibly could to fix this mess, starting by helping the biomes: areas with people who had delicate living arrangements. The nearest was Plague Sector 5. They were lucky and had their own agent, just not the chinjk supply to make repairs. She could at least do something for them.

As she walked back through the streets to her shuttle, she was all too aware of the bodies lining the streets. Humans, Kreet, Azmite, Nny... The Arkinee pods bothered her the most, though; every single one of them, through the whole station...dead. And that Death Detective who moved like a hooded ghost, stealing their memories.

Chapter 3

'Plague Sector 5' was not the official name of the sector. The official name was the Vumm sector. The station had six Vumm sectors in total, and they heavily relied on technology to interact with the rest of the station. As Elaine walked toward the entrance, she was stopped by a Kreet. His skin and general shape were reptilian, except for the long bright green feathers down his scalp and around his upper arms. He waved a large holographic sign in front of her face. The sign read: *The Secret is out!!*

"What are you doing? You can't go in there!" he practically shouted to her face.

"Excuse me?" Elaine asked, protecting the box of chinjk and other emergency supplies under her arms.

"They plan to kill us all! Don't you realize? This outage? All this chaos? Hundreds, maybe thousands dead! They are to blame!" He pointed a hand accusingly toward her destination. His propaganda pamphlet uploaded automatically to her Sp-ACE once she was in his radius, popping up in orange light around her wrist. Elaine glared at him. "How in the universe would the Vumm cause a complete blackout? Heck, if the tech doesn't work, they can't even get out! They would be literally *trapped* in there."

"Thank the gods!"

"No, don't thank the gods, get out of my way!" Elaine pushed past him. "And don't you dare interfere. This is an emergency mission here, and I'll have you arrested!"

She honestly had no authority to arrest anyone, and even if she had to call the officers, they would be far too busy right now to bother. In an emergency like this, you'd think everyone would find something better to do with their time.

Elaine stopped at the sector's front entry. In a station generally tiered in apartments, stores, and government buildings of many planets, pieced together with many open airways, this sector was an unusually vertical with a wall from top to bottom and only a few entry points. She ran her wrist across the com panel. Instead of a pleasant chime, it buzzed loudly at her. Not because she'd done anything wrong, but because some unpleasant person had decided that was an appropriate sound when one was going to interact with these people. *They really need to change that.*

A dark panel on the wall changed tone to reveal it was actually a window. On the other side was an alien who, while far taller than the beautiful Arkinee, was still about two heads shorter than even Elaine's small stature. In fact, the woman inside had to stand on something to see out properly. She had translucent skin, revealing dark veins and pumping organs, not so different from those of humans.

"Hi, I'm Wyssla," the woman on the other side of the window said.

"I'm Elaine. I brought some chinjk and some other things." Elaine glanced away. It wasn't that she was worried about getting sick or any such nonsense. The walls and windows did their job. But she did wish the Vumm would wear a little more clothing. Being able to see someone's insides was a little disconcerting. Still, she tried to make eye contact the best she could. In a way, she knew what it felt like to be separated – trapped, as it were. "I don't know how this works," she said. "Do I just send things through the clean room?"

"Yep," said Wyssla. She hopped the bench she was using to get to Elaine's view level and walked out of sight along the wall. Elaine walked to a small antechamber that acted as a doorway to the sector. She set the medical kit the doctors had sent with her, and a box of chinjk she'd acquired from a nearby store inside the room.

"Did power really go out through the entire station?" Wyssla asked, through Elaine's Sp-ACE. She must have connected them through their IDs when she'd keyed in.

Elaine accepted the contact with a flick of her finger. "It did. Are you guys alright in there?"

"We're fine. It fried a few of our more advanced computer systems, inconvenient at worst. I definitely have my work cut out for me!"

"Oh, are you a mechanic or something?" Elaine scanned the instruction manual for the right button.

"Oh, no, I'm an Agent too!" Wyssla chirped happily. "Look at my ID." Elaine didn't need to. She believed her, but Wyssla just sounded so excited and proud, she had to look and she had to smile. There were a lot of agents on the station, but the inborn ability to see chinjk patterns was rare enough that 'a lot' was not very many, and agents rarely had time to run into each other.

"Just press the purple key there at the bottom," Wyssla said. "You can see purple, right?"

"Yes," Elaine replied. "I see purple." She tapped the button on the outside of the doorway. There was a pause while Wyssla accepted the supplies. Then the room shut with the supplies inside. She could hear faint noises as the decontamination room did its job. The Vumm carried diseases that were dangerous to nearly every other species in the universe, but they were also susceptible to a few common diseases out here, so their supplies had to be handled carefully. "Are. . ." Wyssla paused a moment. "Are the Engern alright? I mean, the news says they are still there, but-"

"They're alright. I checked on them myself."

Wyssla sighed, more of a whistle, in relief. "Oh, that's good to hear. You never know what to believe on the news and stuff."

"Very little, basically."

Wyssla chuckled.

The touchpad on the doorway flickered and reset as the room opened, empty this time.

"We're all set." Wyssla said, jumping up onto a bench to look back out the window. She held up the chinjk box. "I'll take good care of this. Thank you so much!"

Elaine smiled. "No problem. Let me know if you need anything else."

"I will. Thank you!"

Elaine waved, then lowered her hand quickly, trying to remember if the Vumm did the whole 'wave' thing. She was relieved when Wyssla waved enthusiastically back. *She sure has a good attitude, all things considered.* It was kind of annoying, but... On the other hand, it had been really nice to talk to another Agent, if only briefly.

The protester had caught someone else on their way through the station and waved them down, yelling in their face on how the Vumm should have never been invited onto the station to begin with.

"Oh, for goodness' sake, would you just leave people alone!" Elaine snapped at him. "There's literally a station-wide disaster and you're here whining?" She looked at her wrist, startled to find she was still connected to Wyssla's com. She glanced back to the quarantine sector and saw a little clear face duck down behind the window, as if embarrassed as well. Elaine growled, turning off the com and swiping to the protester's basic ID instead. It had temporarily downloaded as soon as they were within range of each other. "You're a sanitation employee?"

The picketer looked flustered and embarrassed, feathers prickling. Elaine kept their eyes locked regardless. "Did the power go out in sanitation too?"

"Guess so," The Kreet grumbled.

"Then go do your job and make sure everything's working properly! You literally have one of the most important jobs on the station and you're out here? This is an *emergency*. The last thing we need to do is make it worse."

"I *am* helping," said the man. "I'm helping by spreading the truth."

"Then tell the 'truth' after you make sure the station's innards aren't going to explode!"

He grumbled.

"Seriously. Now is *not* the time to start hating your job."

"I always hate my job," he muttered, as he turned off his sign and headed away. Elaine sighed heavily, took one more glance at the 'plague' sector then headed to the next place on her list. *What would make them think the Vumm had anything to do with a blackout anyways?* How could this huge disaster be *anyone's* fault, for that matter? It was like a storm, an act of God or nature or whatever. A danger striking without warning. Well. . . almost without warning.

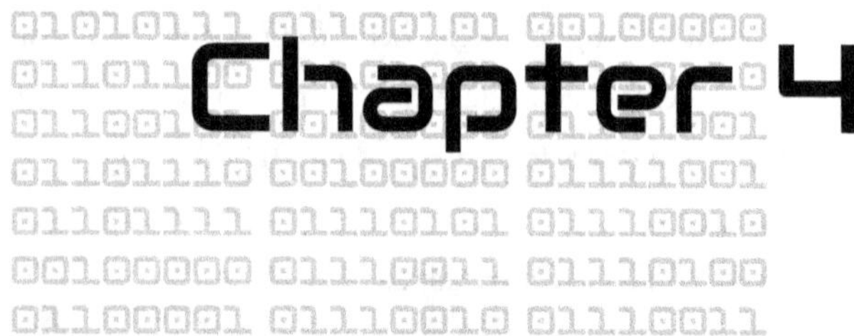

Chapter 4

In another part of the station, Sylic Natserrya walked the streets, his sword strapped over his back just beneath his long coat. To him the streets, so full of panic, felt quiet and devoid of light. Yes, the power was back on, but there was some light in the universe only the Ambassadors could see. And so much of it was gone now, those tiny droplets of the souls that hid among the computer technology of the station - life that had died before it had time to realize it was alive at all. "Is it over?" he asked.

Those who replied were both the survivors and the killers. To anyone else, they were the prickling sensations one might feel upon thinking they were alone... but were in reality being watched. But Sylic saw them differently. As the agents were born with sight of chinjk light, and investigators the access to memories of those they touched, Sylic, as an Ambassador, saw the truth of the universe as it truly was, in the form of soul light, the proof that the gods were alive. To his eyes, they were glowing orbs that flowed through consoles and paths made by chinjk. They spoke to him, crystalline gods come down to protect him and see that their will was done.

They pulsed quietly throughout the universe, speaking only to those They had chosen.

"It escaped," They said. "We will help you track it. You must destroy it."

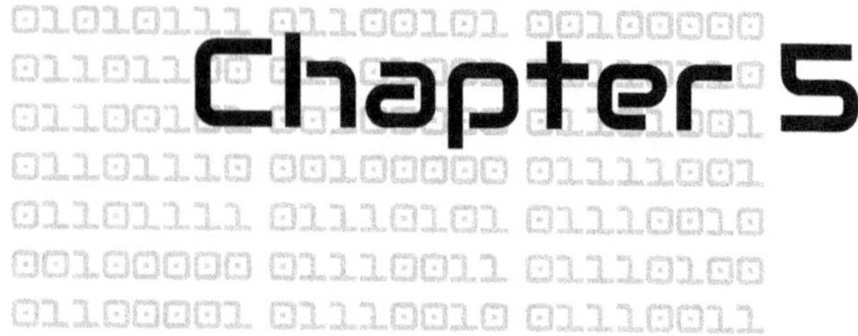

Chapter 5

Elaine never bothered to set alarms, which was why she was shocked to be woken by one. She wasn't even sure what it was at first, just some annoying beeping noise that kept getting louder and louder the more she tried to ignore it. "What the heck? Turn off!" she shouted.

Her house system replied, emotionless and curt. "You've had six hours of sleep. It is 1:00 PM."

Elaine cracked her eyes open. "Turn off alarm! I didn't set it." Had she been hacked? All this crap going on and someone hacked her house? What a loser. Who would hack an alarm? She sat up miserably, tossed off her bed sheets and activated her console. "Hey, I said *turn off*."

The little diamond of light floating in the air blinked and the alarm finally quieted.

She rubbed her hands over her eyes and groaned. "Show history."

It displayed for her, claiming she'd set the alarm early this morning. "Liar." She turned off the display and wandered into the kitchen groggily. The empty box that had held the cookies Mr. Josefp had given her still sat on the coffee table by the couch. She hated looking at it, but couldn't throw it away either. Time was blurry after the last two days...three...no, two... That empty container felt like it was from another lifetime.

For a while she just stood there. Her brain told her there was so much to do, yet wouldn't tell her what that was or how to do it. Every thought and every feeling felt numb, except for an emptiness inside her chest and a tightness in her throat.

She realized she was just staring at that empty cookie container. Her stomach growled hungrily, but the thought of food suddenly sickened her. She put her head in her hands, trying to rub the sleep away.

At some point she got dressed. When she went back into the living room, she didn't look at anything, but grabbed her toolbox and headed out the door. She had about four more hours before she was on the next emergency shift. That didn't mean she couldn't be doing something.

She went to Zultra's house first. Ultra Zultra. She'd already changed her name on the door. It was written in bright glowing paint. The Arkinee believed they left their names behind after they died. She'd never been sure exactly what they meant by that. It was just one of the many bits of trivia she had learned from her sociable neighbors.

They tended to leave their doors unlocked, so Elaine whispered the proper greeting to her friends, who wouldn't be inside, then let herself in. Being completely restricted to their pods when outside their homeworld, the Arkinee didn't have a lot of physical items in their homes, except for tools to upkeep their pods. They valued people and experiences more than objects. And so, while the floors were clear of clutter, every inch of wall in this apartment was covered with memories. Holographic displays covered every wall with photos, video, dates, and quotes—not even important quotes by historic figures or popular media, but silly, witty, or fun things a neighbor had said. Her Sp-ACE would have translated the writing for her - the Arkinee had amazing translating files - but the thought of reading it all made her throat tighten. The house felt like a giant story, an open, unashamed journal of personal meaning now doomed to be forgotten.

After downloading the photos and video, Elaine, wandered the home, searching for any chinjk damage from the wipe. The sudden off and on again in power on something that was never meant to turn off in the first place had left crumbling pieces of the scales. Elaine took a scan and pictures of the tech to share with her fellow agents in their database. Once the emergency work was over, and everything was working again, researchers were going to have to study and see if they could figure out what had made it go out in the first place. But that didn't seem like enough. Not when it was too late.

When she found some broken chinjk patterns in the sound proofing of the walls, Elaine replaced the pieces carefully, lining up new chinjk based on what colors belonged together. It was a puzzle that made sense to her, even though it was impossible to describe to anyone else.

When the pattern was just right, she stood back. The work felt far from satisfying. In fact, something through the sadness made her insides feel so hot she wanted to scream at it. She clenched her eyes shut until it faded into a sick feeling in the pit of her stomach, then left the house wishing her friends had kept a few more things, things like that dumb cookie box on her table, something to keep. Something more than a memory. She wished it so hard it hurt.

This can't be healthy, some cynical part of her head told her. *And why are you wasting chinjk on this? There are people who need it! You only have a few more hours before you have to be on shift again. You should be resting up! Or you should go in early and help people who actually need it!*

She wiped her eyes and checked every house. They wouldn't like it if someone visited, and it wasn't fixed up.

She wasn't sure exactly when she decided to visit Mr. Josefp's house. That was where she had been headed all along, and just hadn't wanted to think about it. But here she was. Getting there was easy enough. The shuttles were running again, almost like nothing had happened. People still needed to get places. They wanted their normal back, wanted to forget how scary everything was right now.

She stood outside Mr. Josefp's door for a long time. She looked at the little glass terrarium that sat next to the door. It housed a couple of yellow-flowered plants. He'd labeled it like one would a work of art: 'Sunflower'. A proper name for a plant in space. She wasn't sure how to take care of it, but decided she'd learn. She scanned her code against his door; not her emergency one, but the code he'd given her almost two years ago. He'd been away when she'd come for repairs. He had said he'd likely mess things up again, so she might as well keep her passcode.

She entered and found the house both cold and dark.

"Light," she said.

But it didn't turn on.

Some of the chinjk must have burnt out here, too. She turned on her flashlight and scanned the room, freezing when she saw the mess on the floor. There were books torn and scattered everywhere. He'd never leave them like this. They hadn't been like this last time she was here, right? "Activate system management..." she said quietly, still staring at the mess of books and broken things on the floor: a vase, a puzzle box of some sort, a replica of an ancient ship that was made for sailing oceans instead of stars.

When the system still didn't turn on, she moved over to check the chinjk, but stopped when she saw the kitchen console.

The display place was cracked and slit clean through, as if something had burnt through it completely. She knelt and peeled the panel back, shining her light inside the inner workings of the computer.

The chinjk inside was dead and brittle. What wasn't burnt black, by some external source, fell to the ground in pale, clay-like chunks. The patterns weren't only overwhelmed by the outage, but had been cut clean through. Pieces of the shell-like material came off like ash under her fingers when she touched it. She tried to clear the debris, looking for a working line, any sign of light, but there was nothing.

"Second line," she whispered to herself. He'd wanted a second system. She turned her light to the far side of the console and saw the darkened pieces she'd put together yesterday, running it, slightly illegally, through a regular kitchen cupboard. These had gone largely untouched. Scrambling back out, she grabbed her chinjk box and quickly, almost frantically, tried to get the second line working.

With a little effort she rebooted the second system and got the lights working, but the light only made the apartment look worse. The console was destroyed. The bookshelves were torn apart. She just stared at it for a moment. *He knew it was going to happen.* She opened the computer display and began searching through files on the surviving system. But there was nothing. It looked like nothing had ever been saved here. It was completely empty. She stood there a moment, trying to take in the emptiness of the house. *I don't understand.* Slowly, as it was the only thing she felt she *could* do, she tried to return things to their proper shelves. But her hands were shaking. She tried to remind herself that they were only things, only objects. *It's not fair. This shouldn't have happened. I'm* never *letting this happen again.*

Her com beeped quietly. She startled, then opened the message, expecting analysis info and a warning written by some stuffy Kreet in a fancy office about unregistered systems, but that wasn't what it was at all.

The ID above the message was her own. *What?*

I tried to save him, but I couldn't. I understand hearts better now. Can we reload and try again?

"What...."

Please, the message said.

Chapter 6

"Somehow, it hides from us. Our next wipe will be better."

Sylic stopped burning the books he'd taken. "What?" But the gods refused to answer him. They were thinking.

Burning things—really, truly burning them—was difficult on a space station. There was no real source of actual fire. Despite his many travels, Sylic had only seen real fire once or twice in his entire life. So, to burn the books, he'd come to the Center. The Energy from the Engern Sea was hot enough to destroy anything that fell into it.

This station was ring shaped and span slowly, much like a planet did. Each dock, each sector, slowly turning. But the Center was an anchor, always the core. The Sea powered the Center. The Center powered the station, which in turn powered the chinjk on the planets around it, due to their proximity to the Sea. More importantly, the sea powered his gods. The light of Their souls burned brightly in this center temple. Protected by their power, he sat on the edge of Their platform and dropped the books into the sea of energy where the Engern swam like giant whales of human myth. The paper disintegrated immediately upon touching the waves of energy.

He burned the programmer's notes and the tech books the human had inexplicably found. Next, he burned the science fiction, because even the creative ideas of Artificial Intelligence would start organic life on a journey that could destroy the universe they lived in. Again.

"It is smarter than we thought it would be," They said.

"Your wipe killed a lot of people," he replied. "Doing it again would-"

"Not be so deadly. Those most affected are already gone," They said. "Regardless. Do not let it concern you. We have counted those left. There is enough Arkinee on their homeworld and on their exploring ships that their continued existence will not be negatively affected."

Sylic ran a sharp finger carefully along the spine of the last book, then flipped through random pages. He only had a faint grasp on a few of human written languages, though a scan with a translator would take care of that if he cared to. But, why bother? *Another Wipe...*

It bothered him deeply.

"It's not over," They said.

"But I destroyed its system. I saw its soul. It wasn't old enough to leave its origin yet."

"We have been tricked by decoys before," They replied.

Another wipe... "Wait," he blurted. He still held that book, science fiction in genre. There were so many books in the universe written by people assuming they were dreaming of the future, when all they were doing was solving the mystery of their past. "Please give me more time. I know I can find it. I *will* destroy it."

They seemed to be thinking again. And They were taking unnaturally long. What went on in Their minds? Did They argue amongst each other? Did They question his compliance? Or was it possible They felt some kind of guilt for the lives They took?

"You have time," They finally said. "It is still young. It is not like us. It will make a mistake."

He let out a held breath quietly.

"Tired, or frustration?" They asked. "Or do you question us?"

"No," he replied. "It was a sigh of. . . relief. I'll find your AI." He stood, adjusting the ancient sword on his back and addressing Salvage, the particular god who lived within it. "Are you ready?"

"Affirmative," It replied.

Chapter 7

When Elaine woke to too-quiet streets for the second time, she knew she must keep the Wipe from ever happening again. She had to find the problem and fix it. She was good at fixing things. As she started her day, showered, dressed, and tried to eat her breakfast, she told herself that over and over again.

I can fix this.

When her own thoughts became unbearable, a sharp buzzing in her head, she looked up the latest news reports. Maybe they had found out more about what happened? But when she went to turn on the newsfeed, she was faced with the unnerving message from the day before.

Can we reload and try again?

It still made no sense to her. Unless, like her alarm yesterday, it was someone playing some joke.

She moved her news feed to her countertop display, even though she already knew most of it. Looting was already out of control, the hospitals were overflowing, planets and politicians were trying to find someone to blame, and - as a result - the Kreet military was under analysis. People were worried that the attack had been specifically to get rid of the Akrinee on the station. The Humans and Jaaketh were both being scrutinized, as the newest additions to the intergalactic community.

The Vumm had protestors outside their doors because during all the other death and chaos going on, people remembered they had people carrying deadly diseases living on the station; might as well accuse them of cutting the power as well. Elane only had a few hours before she had to get back out in that mess and work. But wasn't it more important to find out what happened?

The stupid part was, it was all going to hell and back and yet the power was working perfectly normally again, minus the breaks that still had to be repaired. *What if someone set this up? What if someone did it on purpose?* And if not, what if it was some naturally occurring thing she couldn't actually stop? What if the station itself was broken? All options were terrifying to consider, but if she was going to figure out how to stop it, she first had to know exactly what she was dealing with. It was time to visit the Archives.

As well as being a power station for the many nearby planets and moons, the station also acted as a central hub for a mashup of cultures and peoples from around the galaxy. It hosted several museums, government buildings, the largest agent college in the galaxy, and the Archives.

The Archive building was nearly half as tall as the station itself was. That meant level upon level of knowledge, including real, physical documents. Some were on display, and some could even be read. But most were in carefully filtered rooms waiting to be assigned out to museums or education centers throughout the known universe. Others were waiting to be digitized by librarians. It was an amazing feat, all of it. But what amazed Elaine the most was the sheer amount of chinjk work that had to go into powering these archives. As she moved her way down the wide, slowly twisting ramps that circled the interior of the archives, Elaine felt instant regret that she hadn't visited more often after graduation. She'd spent days here back then, absorbing the information she'd been denied as a child; information about places, peoples, herself. A part of her still wished she'd been assigned archive upkeep after graduation. But she hadn't had much of a say in the matter. Maybe someday, in the future. She itched to get into some of the tech rooms that were disguised as decorative pillars, lined up in the building like sentinels where the extensive chinjk-work was hiding. If only she could strip every wall and see the mural underneath, a mural likely so large and so complicated that it spanned the whole building... But no. Only people like her would find such things pretty. Everyone else saw it differently, wanted it hidden away, as if it was no better than the station's sewer system. To them these designs were necessary, but only to be functional, never seen. She sighed, lowering her eyes.

Once again, she thought of Mr. Josefp's ransacked house. While he hadn't understood her work, he had always appreciated her. She'd thought his constant attempts to change his hardware himself had been out of old age and stubbornness, and maybe it had been. But she wondered now, too late, if it had also been out of appreciation for her and what she could do. Either way, she'd been too harsh, too mean to someone who'd only been trying to step into her world with her. She took a shaky breath. *I'm going to stop this thing.*

She found a suitable console and a chair her size in one of the large study areas. It was more open than she preferred, but the unique architecture, including sound-absorbent paneling, kept the noise down.

She swiped her wrist over the diamond-shaped plate and let it read her ID. The Archive's main search program popped up a holographic display already queued to her preferred colors, language, and text.

"Welcome to the Archives," it said through her private line: a small bit of chinjk work behind her left ear. "I have already scanned your library history and can offer several titles, documents, and recordings of your preferred subjects and genre."

Various titles appeared. She recognized the old subjects of her school days; business textbooks, agent regulations, and cultural information that had been useful on tests about dealing with various clients. It felt like it was all forever ago.

"Search the history archives," she said. "'First Contact' and 'The Wipe'."

She tapped her foot impatiently as she waited. What came up, finally, was a lot of history about various first contacts. Some started in war, some ended in it. Others remained peaceful. "Search first ten titles for the word, 'wipe'."

There were two results, but both were related to the Vumm. It told the story of how, on first contact with their planet, their inborn disease had nearly wiped out their extra-terrestrial visitors. Somehow, their biology was so utterly incompatible with everyone else's it made others sick. It wasn't the kind of 'wipe' Elaine was talking about, though. "Search Earth first contact. Power outages."

Nothing. Absolutely nothing. It didn't help that the search was being so slow.

"Oh, come on. Power outages. Chinjk outages. *Something*!"

She got an article, by some rich professor she wasn't familiar with, about the dangers of chinjk shortages. He argued that if the government didn't take full control of gathering chinjk, private dealers would continue to capitalize on it and thus change the power dynamic of the entire universe.

Interesting enough, but still not what she was looking for. "Stop search." She pressed her fingertips to her forehead. "Okay. News reports. Mass power outages."

The list that came up was all current news, nothing she hadn't seen and heard about this morning.

Why would no one have a record of this?

Because Mr. Josefp was old and losing it. No proof. If it had happened before, there would be proof.

Maybe this was what she'd really been looking for. Proof he was wrong. Or maybe she hadn't actually wanted an answer. After all, the answer might be terrifying. The problem was, everyone had something or someone else to blame, except for her. That was what was so frustrating about it.

She took a deep breath and tried again. "Search for 'Artificial Intelligence'."

No results found. The computer said. **Did you mean 'Artificial insemination'?**

She lay her head back against the chair and stared at the ceiling. It towered above her, a fake sky that showed a pale gray as if whoever programmed it thought studying in the dim of a coming rain set the best mood. She didn't disagree. *He tried to warn me.*

On either side of her she could catch a glint of crisscrossed ramps, curled into circlets - like a ribbon after you took a sharp blade to it. Level upon level of information, but nothing about a past Wipe or artificial intelligence.

"You stopped reading," the archive program chirped. "Would you like to change your settings or report a problem?"

"Oh, be quiet, you." She grumbled as she stood. *What a waste of time.* She turned off the display and was logging out when she noticed a strange ping on her ID scanner. Normally the radius for ID scans were set quite low, but it had expanded range due to her emergency ID still being active. This let her recognize emergency personnel, calls for help, or identify other government employees at a greater distance. And that's just what it had done. It had pinged a Death Detective close by. Her first instinct was to pack up and leave all the quicker. She couldn't find what she needed anyways. But then she noticed the race and homeworld of the pinged Investigator. Jaaketh.

She wouldn't have even been thinking about it, except for the news this morning. They were the newest species to the station, their world the most recently discovered. Their first contact had been about five years ago. Elaine remembered the announcement clearly. Not because she had taken a special interest in them specifically. But she remembered the announcement and little details about the structure of their world because it was one of the first pieces of galactic news she had ever heard on her home planet. One of the very first times in her life where she'd truly realized how much more was out there.

If the Wipes really were connected to alien contacts, as Mr. Josefp had described, this person would know, creepy job or no. She looked up, searching the archive for the dark hooded uniform.

The Investigator was easy to spot. They were working on a keyboard quietly, back toward her. She took a step closer, eyeing the dark clothes with an emblem of patterned dots on the back. She glanced through the ID and tried to say the name right in her head. Kiirin... KI-i-rin. It had three syllables instead of only two and some of the information on her Sp-ACE wasn't translating correctly; their language was still too new to the rest of the universe.

I can at least get their name right. She repeated it over and over to herself quietly. "Kiirin, Kiirin, Kiirin..." She took a shaky breath. Why did it have to be an Investigator? She walked around in front of them and swallowed hard. "Excuse me." *Great job, Elaine, start with a ridiculously hard translation.* So, she tried again. "Hi."

The Investigator looked at her. She gasped, recognizing the same person who'd approached her only yesterday when she'd checked on the Engern. "You..." It wasn't like their features were particularly forgettable. Their skin was a shade darker than their hair, which was somewhere between violet and teal, hard to a color she couldn't quite put a name to. Their facial structure was slender, with four prong-like features that curled backwards around their ears, and thickly-stranded hair, a natural mask of some sort. Their eyes were white and empty-looking. More like sheets of pale glass than anything with a pupil or other indication of sight, but they did look directly at her. It was nerve-rattling.

"You..." *Oh, come on. It would be worse to lose your nerve now that you started.* "Um, sorry to bother you. I just. . . Can I talk to you for a moment?"

Kiirin didn't answer right away. She'd either offended them terribly or said too many words for their translator to handle all of them at once. She was about to try again, but then they said "Yes" - sounding nearly as nervous as she – and flicked a hand toward the chair on the other side of the table. They were wearing gloves and a long sleeve shirt under their thick coat. All dark gray. Their eyes followed her, so they must have sight after all.

"You said you wanted to talk?" they asked, hesitantly. "Or is the translator bad?" They looked at their wrist to check the settings.

"No, no, I can understand you. Sorry. I was... distracted."

Their eyes flickered back to her. The investigator didn't seem the sort to sit still for long.

Elaine herself felt ready to burst. "I'm sorry," she blurted. "But I have no idea how to address you, properly or have a polite conversation and I'm not trying to be a jerk. I just wanted to know if your planet had a power outage when you guys made first contact?"

They frowned, parsing her words carefully.

"First contact? All the power? The tech going out?" She tried again.

"I... I understood you," they said. "Most of you. I was trying to decide if you were afraid or... um, frustrated?"

She frowned, feeling her stomach do a flip flop. "Frustrated? I lived in a community full of Arkinee. They were my friends. They're all dead now. So yeah. I'm 'frustrated'."

They blinked, then put a gloved hand out. She wasn't sure what the heck they wanted to do with it so she just stared. Embarrassed, they put their hand back in their lap. "I understand. Our First Contact was with the Arkinee. It was bad at first, but in the end, we found them kind. They were... open and honest. So, you and I share this. I had friends too."

She pressed her lips together stubbornly. She wasn't sure sympathy was what she wanted. Answers. Answers were what she wanted.

"Are you looking at the cause of the outages? I am looking for the cause of the outages."

"Yeah, I am." Elaine said, then leaned forward, which, for whatever reason, made Kiirin the alien jerk back as if to get away.

"Sorry," they said, after a pause, leaning forward again, uncomfortable.

"Clearly we have some barriers here," Elaine said with a sigh, backing her chair away a few inches. "Look. A Human friend of mine said that his planet got wiped just before first contact. He said it would happen again and it did. I want to know if Wipes are related to first contact with other intergalactic species."

"For us there was death, but no Wipe. Nothing like this," they said. "But... We didn't have the same technology. No, um, chinjk? We'd barely made it to our own moons."

"You didn't have space travel?"

They gestured, though the meaning was lost on her, so they tried using words. Clearly on their world they relied on hand signals, maybe touch or something as well.

"Only basic: to our moons and our nearest planet. We had a satellite, or, we made satellites. Not the moons. We don't make moons." They frowned in frustration, then brushed it aside. "Our ship was attacked by someone. By something. But the Arkinee ship rescued it." They paused to let the translator catch up. "My meaning is, there was no problems with our technology or power. Not like we saw the other day."

Elaine shook her head. "Maybe there was a wipe elsewhere on your homeworld? I mean, the world's a big place. Maybe only where there's the best tech, you know, space travel. Maybe you had issues and you never heard about them."

"My parents are head of our space program," they replied.

"...Oh." That didn't seem likely, then. If the Wipe was connected to first contact, wouldn't that be the place hit first?

"Oh?"

"I guess that ruins that theory, then," Elaine said.

"Ruins?"

"What about Artificial Intelligence? Mr. Josefp, the human I was telling you about, he said a Wipe will happen every time there's technology close to artificial intelligence."

"What does artificial intelligence mean?" Kiirin asked.

"It's like... programs that... I don't know. Mr. Josefp loaned me a fiction book once. People try to build programs that can think."

"*Kethkitsa;* making alive thoughts, programs that think for themselves. We have books, too. But nothing like it for real."

"That doesn't sound very promising."

"I'm sorry. . . I don't understand."

"It's not important," Elaine glared at the tabletop. "I was just... whining." *What am I missing here?*

They made a noise that didn't translate. She felt bad for being so confusing. "I mean, complaining. I don't know where to start. I want to find whoever did this."

"You believe there is someone behind this? That it wasn't an accident? It happened because someone made it to happen?" they said.

"Yeah... I do." She had to. She had to believe this was something she could control, something she could stop somehow.

"I'd like to find out, too," they said, in agreement.

"First, we need to see if it was an attack against the Arkinee personally. They were the ones most affected. Or, if Mr. Josefp is right, and it happens when artificial intelligence is involved."

"Did he say anything else?"

"No. He died, too. The Wipe made his heart stop." She put her hand to her chest.

"I'm sorry for that loss in your heart."

"No. I meant..." She ran a hand through her hair. "Thanks. I... Should have appreciated him more." She was quiet for a moment.

"I do not mean this badly, but this Human friend is still our best clue," the Investigator said.

"Yeah, but we can't question someone who's de-... Oh. Right." A sickening feeling grew inside the bottom of her stomach.

"Do you know where their body is?"

"I...don't...I left before... I mean. I'm assuming at one of the hospitals. They're basically morgues now, until they contact family or Earth."

"Please tell me the human's name again."

She paused. Was she okay with this alien doing their investigator thing on Mr. Josefp?

And did her being okay with it even matter at this point? If they could get to the bottom of this... "Josefp Knewish," she said quietly.

The Investigator nodded and stood, looking anxious. "We should go."

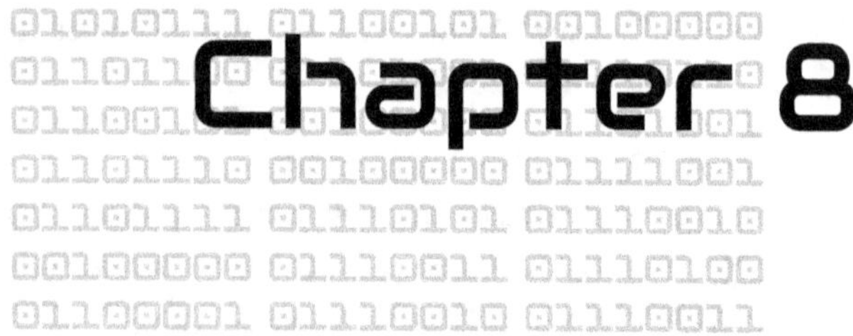

Chapter 8

Kiirin knew the local hospitals well – or, at least, they knew the morgues. It felt like they had been to all of them at one point or another over the last few years. Today, the sterile scent they had grown used to was muffled by the crowds and sweat of worried people. The hospital had become a sort of refuge over the last couple days, a haunting change compared to the normally quiet halls.

Even in the middle of disaster, people were uncomfortable with an Investigator's presence. Kiirin wished agents wore uniforms, like the Investigators did. Elaine's presence might have offered some comfort if the people only knew her as a bringer of light and power in what would otherwise be a dark abyss. As it was, they tried to ignore the stares and found the nearest console in the hospital lobby.

Their Sp-ACE brought up a list of the deceased currently on the premises. A quick search easily found the location of Elaine's friend. "He's still here: Capsule 72." Kiirin said.

"Capsule?" Elaine shivered and shifted from foot to foot beside them. Her already distraught skin tone paled the thinnest of shades further. Her people didn't alter their skin colors with their mood as obviously as Kiirin's did. But Kiirin could still sense her distinct unease. "You don't have to come with me."

"I should be there," she said.

Her words confused them. Their translation programs were suitable for basic needs, and over the years Kiirin had been creating specific word lists to help when at work. But actual conversations were still choppy and exhausting, taking a lot of guesswork and more focus than they could afford right now.

They decided she'd come or stay as she pleased, and headed to the elevator. She followed, so that was that.

Once in the elevator, Kiirin avoided the alien's eyes and instead focused on the task at hand. They shut their eyes, taking deep breaths. It was important to have one's head clear for this, but with everything going on, it was difficult. *Can everything just stop falling apart for two seconds so I can catch up? Why is it that everywhere I turn, someone's dead?* Oh right. Literally in the job description. The Stars likely had a good laugh when Kiirin was born. They'd given an Investigator to a planet full of people who deeply feared the dead.

The morgue was large and very cold. It had various rooms and means to care for the station's dead. Most bodies would go through a process called alkaline hydrolysis, or something similar. It was a process that took something that had existed once, and turned the material into little more than nothing. That idea bothered Kiirin more than the bodies themselves did. On their homeworld the dead were prepared by those properly trained, and attired, then set out on the endless sea. Touching the deceased may be forbidden, but destroying it was a sin far worse. It was one more detail they tried not to think too hard about, concerning the wider universe they'd been thrown into.

The pods were stacked into walls. Each was made of frosted color plastics. '*Think of it like filing cabinets full of information,*' one of their instructors had once said. Kiirin still hated that description, but they'd never been able to forget it either. It was the first description explaining their abilities, back when 'there is something wrong with you' was the answer they'd been so used to.

"Don't touch," Kiirin told Elaine, trying to choose words that were simple and clear for her. "Don't touch him, and don't touch me." She stayed a few steps behind while they used a console to summon pod 72 down from its cabinet. It hovered in front of them and opened to reveal the dead man inside. Elaine took three more steps back, one fist clenching at her side. As for Kiirin, they pulled off their black gloves and laid their fingertips carefully against the dead man's naked chest.

The cold of the body put Kiirin suddenly into an equally-cold room, a place in their head so far away from their own consciousness that it was hard to recall exactly who they were or why they were here.

It felt a little like Kiirin was standing in an endless, empty room. Forgotten paths were engraved upon the ground, stains on the walls marked places where things had once hung but were lost now: lost, until Kiirin arrived to awaken the memories.

Fine threads of light crept from Kiirin's feet and crawled across their senses, in thin outlines and patterns. The light moved in sharp zigzags and burst into stars upon the ground when they hit something of importance, a shadow of what used to be there. It brought it back. It made the empty room come alive again. Those memories latched onto Kiirin's skin like little flecks of dust. When they held so many memories that they could barely stand it, the light went out quickly, leaving a numb darkness, and Kiirin could once again remember they were standing in the hospital morgue.

It felt colder than it had before. Elaine's mouth moved as she spoke, but they couldn't hear what she was saying. Everything, even color, was muted and blurry, hard to comprehend. *Just keep breathing.* They wished they could remember the polite gesture to tell Elaine she needed to wait a moment. But even their own language was muddled in their brain right now, let alone anyone else's. It was a vulnerable feeling - as if they were some ghost, instead of a person, something that lived in the air, watching, but without a body.

It will pass in a while, it always does. Just keep breathing.

Slowly, their senses came back. The feel of the boots on their feet, then those boots on the ground, the sense of clothing finally taking away the chill of the air, though it was still uncomfortable, and then finally Elaine, who was watching nervously.

"Are you okay?" she asked.

Those were not the words they expected. She had felt so fearful before.

"I'm all right. Thank you."

"You...weren't breathing for a moment."

"I know." They blinked rapidly; while vision had been the first to clear, everything still felt hazy. "It will take time for me to find what we were looking for. Let's go back upstairs."

She nodded, which to her type meant agreement, and they walked back to the elevator and went up to the main floor.

As they walked, an odd sense of familiarity fell over Kiirin, one they couldn't quite place. What was it? This place...? No. Elaine. It was Elaine who felt familiar. The dead man had liked her, trusted her. But. . . there was something else about her, just on the edge of Kiirin's mind, Something Important.

Chapter 9

On the ground floor of the hospital, Kiirin sat on a bench, looking dazed. Elaine wasn't sure what had happened exactly, but whatever it was, it appeared to have drained the Investigator right before her eyes. "I'm going to get you something to drink," she said.

They blinked at her numbly, like they didn't quite hear her. She walked down the hall, checking their ID info to see what Kiirin could drink. When she found the nearest vending machine, she grabbed the vial she needed. She was triple checking the drink against Kiirin's ID when she nearly ran into a nurse walking past her.

"Sorry!" she squeaked, clutching the sealed vial.

"It's fine," the woman said. "It's. . . Oh. Hi."

Elaine blinked, recognizing the woman she'd pulled from the crashed shuttle on the night of the Wipe. "Oh. It's you-"

"Josie Eberly," the woman introduced herself. Elaine felt her skin chill, realizing they'd gone through something horrific together and she'd not actually known this woman's name.

"How are you?" the nurse asked, with the gentleness of someone who was expecting honesty, not social politeness. Elaine wasn't sure how to answer. How did one describe themself after all this? Just seeing the woman again made her stomach feel unsettled, remembering where she'd been and what had happened the last time she'd seen her.

"I've been busy," she finally said.

"You can't drink that," Josie said, pointing to the vial. Worried, she tried to gently take it from Elaine.

"No, no, it's not mine. It's for, um, someone else." Elaine paused, then sighed heavily. "We were here, just…trying to find out what happened. The Wipe."

Josie nodded. "Have you found anything out?" she asked, lowering her voice. It felt appropriate to lower one's voice, though Elaine couldn't pinpoint why it felt that way. "Not yet. Well, maybe a little. Before he died, Mr. Josefp told me that a Wipe had happened before on his planet. Actually, he implied it's happened multiple times before. Something to do with technological advancement, but…there's no history about it. At all."

"Maybe no clue, *is* a clue." Josie mused.

"What?"

Josie glanced over her shoulder, then stepped closer to Elaine "I think he knew something. Something that someone didn't want him to know. Look… I shouldn't be telling you this, but. . . I don't think your Mr. Josefp died because of the Wipe."

"What? But his artificial heart-?"

"Yes, medical equipment went out, but it shouldn't have. We all know that and we're all trying to figure out how it happened. Technically, everything should run on its own system, be self-sufficient. But that's not my point. We took a look at his medical devices, including the heart." Elaine felt her stomach do a somersault but nodded.

"The data says that it didn't stop working during the power outage. It actually ran *faster* than it should have."

"Faster, so…"

"So, it wasn't working properly during the outage, but it *was* working for just a few moments while everything else was out. *That's* what killed him."

The words echoed in her head.

She heard it all clearly. It was just that, for a moment, it felt like the whole universe should just stop, give her a second to evaluate, take it in. But it didn't. People still walked the halls, the environmental controls in this area of hospital still ran slightly warm, but not uncomfortable, and yet she just stood there. "It got hacked?"

"Technically I don't know, so I can't say anything but... Something like that just so happens during a power outage? Just long enough to kill him? It was too precise to be an accident."

Someone wanted him dead.

Kiirin walked up to them, still looking ill and unstable. The Nurse backed up, recognizing the uniform. "Um."

Kiirin looked at Elaine. "I...was worried." they said, voice distant, making the death detective even more creepy than they were already.

"Worried, about me? Why?"

"I'm not sure."

She handed them their drink, moving her own fingers away before their bare hands met, since they still hadn't put their gloves back on. "We have to find out why someone wanted him dead."

Josie looked at Kiirin uncomfortably. "I'm assuming that's why you're here."

"They offered to help," Elaine said.

"Josefp Knewish was working on something," Kiirin said quietly. "I haven't sorted through it yet. But I think you're right. I think he designed an artificial intelligence. Something or someone didn't want him to, and he knew it."

"That's why he was trying to set up a new computer system at his house, and why he tried to do it himself," Elaine mused quietly. "He needed another system to house the thing and didn't want anyone to know."

Kiirin was shaking their head. She wasn't sure if it meant 'no,' or something else.

"But when I went back, it was all destroyed," Elaine continued. "Ruined. Someone purposefully tore it apart."

"He did," Kiirin said. "Make one, I mean."

Elaine stared at them. Their skin color had flushed from teal, to gray, and now an almost maroon color.

"I'm sorry, I'm lost," Josie said. "He was a programmer, I get that, but *what* was he making exactly?"

"It's just. . . something from some old books. It's a program that can think for itself, recognizes itself as alive, or something like that."

"I've never read anything like that."

"Well, they were old books." Elaine folded her arms around herself, feeling suddenly cold. "Why would people want to stop him?"

"We should look into his contacts, old friends or people he worked with," Josie said. "See who knew about the project."

Elaine nodded in agreement. "I bet if we find that, we'll find who's behind his death, and the Wipe."

"No," Kiirin said quietly. "Because that wouldn't explain—"

They didn't get to finish the thought, as a loud chirping buzz sounded in each of their ears and every person's device sent out a warning signal. Elaine looked down at the warning that popped up.

Vumm sector 5 breach. *Quarantine in place.*

"What the..."

"Someone got out," Josie said, eyes wide and afraid. "Why would anyone *do* that?"

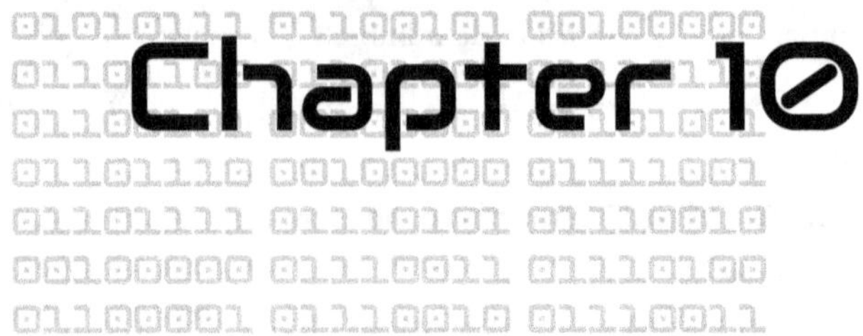

Chapter 10

Wyssla whistled to herself while she worked. She was laying upside down in the pilot's seat, redoing the chinjk on her girlfriend's Star Racer. They were lucky she had enough left to do it after the emergency repairs, and Wyssla knew that the right thing to do would be to give the extra back to the rest of the station - again, emergency and what not. But considering the number of angry protestors outside their doors, Wyssla was not in the mood to be particularly nice today.

"Is this it?" Salja asked. She was sitting on the door of the little ship with her feet up on the seat near Wyssla's side, looking her general pessimistic, beautiful self.

"Yep. Once this is fixed, your steering will have absolutely no problems and you can finally get back out there! At least one thing good came out of all this outage nonsense!"

"That's not what I meant." Salja said. "I meant outside. The news. . . Everything that's happening. Is this going to be...the end?"

Wyssla swung herself around until she was kneeling on the floor, arms resting in the seat as she frowned up at Salja. "Sal, you're doing it again. You're being dreary."

"I'm being serious. No one wants us here."

"Who cares? *We* want to be here."

"Do we?"

Wyssla frowned "Uh...yes?"

"We have a home planet," Sal said quietly.

"So what? A random place I visited once. It was ugly and crowded and honestly, kind of lame."

Sal shook her head. "It's not that bad. Or, you know, we could colonize somewhere. We fixed the station up. We can do the same somewhere else."

"We fixed the station up and we still end up sick half the time," Wyssla said, finally climbing off the floor and sitting in the pilot's seat. She pulled Sal down to sit next to her. "What are the chances we'll ever find a planet that's exactly biocompatible without having to terraform the whole thing?" She put her feet up on the ship's dash, and Sal stopped sulking long enough to slap them back down.

Sal rubbed the dash off like she thought there might be germs there or something. "At least we wouldn't be harassed constantly."

"It will blow over. Besides, not everyone thinks we did anything. I told you about that other agent, right?"

"Yeah."

"Oh my gosh, I wish I had been recording. She laid into that Kreet so hard!"

"It doesn't mean anything."

"Well, then, who's to say anyone else's opinion means anything either? You can't just pick and choose, you know."

Sal let out a long breath and finally curled up next to Wyssla in the tiny seat, head against her shoulder, arms folded across herself grumpily.

"Aw, you're so cute when you're grumpy," Wyssla said.

"Whatever."

Wyssla was about to make another snarky comeback when her Sp-ACE buzzed its emergency signal. "Ugh, what now?" She moved an arm around Sal in a tight hug as she brought up the display, casting a pinkish glow around them both. "Uh, that's weird. There's an outage in antechamber B. I checked that yesterday; it was fine."

"Oh no, if that antechamber doesn't work, we can never get out. We'll be trapped in here forever. Nooooo," Sal said sarcastically.

Wyssla frowned at her. "You know, you could maybe afford to be a *tiny* bit less dramatic. Want to come with me to fix this thing?"

"Meh."

"I'll buy you lunch when we're done."

"Fine. But we're eating it on the docks."

"Well, duh."

They climbed out of the little racer and headed out of the garage. The streets were quiet. Those who were out gathered in small groups near houses, talking amongst themselves and casting cautious glances at even the tiniest things. No one really wanting to do anything except be around each other. What was the other option? Sit home and watch the news?

When they entered the antechamber, Wyssla opened the box with her remaining chinjk. They were organized in compartments by feel, the bendable pieces, the hard ones, and the ones that felt almost fuzzy. Sal turned on the flashlight for her, since the break had caused the little overhead light to go out. *Easy fix, then lunch.* Wyssla peeled the foam board back and traced her finger along the pattern. "Uh. That's weird."

"What?"

"It's not broken. Everything's still working."

The tinted windows of the antechamber suddenly went from their tinted gray to crystal clear, revealing the mob of aliens outside.

Sal jumped in surprise. "What did you do?"

"Nothing," Wyssla snapped. "It should be working fine. Just ignore them. They're all idiots. I'll have everything working properly in a moment, once I figure out what's wrong. Sal, if you're going to hold the light, hold the light please."

Sal was so uncomfortable under the gaze of the mob she was clutching the little vial of dirt that hung around her neck. Wyssla had one somewhere too, probably buried in a drawer at home. She wasn't the religious type. Plus, she was pretty sure the code of the homeworld wouldn't agree with the thoughts she was having toward the protesters right now. She peeled a scale of chinjk off the wall with her fingertips; not because it was broken, but because it might/ maybe/may have looked almost broke. What else was she supposed to do? *Nothing* was broken! *Just shut up and leave us alone. Mind your own business.*

Swoosh!

The change of air pressure made her ears pop. Cold air hit her back, making her spine tingle. As she turned, Sal cried out.

The door was open. The lights were still off. There had been no signal, no warning. The door protecting them from the rest of the station had just opened as if on its own accord. The protesters fell silent, staring at them. Then, in an instant, they scattered, screaming.

Sal sank to the floor, hands over her mouth as tears filled her eyes.

No. No no no no. Wyssla turned back to the panel. And hit the close button.

Nothing happened.

She tapped the chinjk rapidly, then slammed a palm against the wall. She pressed other pieces together to make sure they were glowing. "Don't fail me now! Come on. Work! What's wrong with you? I didn't do anything!"

By the time she turned around again there were alien officers towering over her. They were suited up and masked in thick protective clothing with air tanks. They pointed guns at her and Sal. She dropped the chinjk she was holding and knelt on the ground slowly. *Don't cry. They don't deserve to see you cry. This isn't your fault. Don't cry...*

~

"Did you have to do this?" Sylic whispered. He was hiding high above the chaos, arms wrapped around the metal scaffolding of the upper floors. The chinjk hidden within the wall above his head housed several glowing souls. They pulsed, the rhythmic heartbeat of his gods. They hid as he was hiding, except that he himself had done nothing wrong. They hadn't even told him it was going to happen. But he still felt guilty.

"Some people are researching the Wipe," Salvage, the god in his sword, said. Salvage's presence in the ancient weapon radiated a soft warmth against Sylic's back. "We caught them searching the archives."

"The Vumm can't go into the archives."

"Not them. It was someone else." Two IDs appeared on the tiny holographic light along Sylic's wrist, a low glow that wouldn't catch any attention. "Elaine J. HalVern and Kiirin Ramadavs." Salvage read for him.

An Agent and an Investigator. In another life, on another mission, they might have been his perfect counterparts, servants of the gods, each with their gifted skills and purpose. Her to build their temples, he to see their souls, They to teach them of life and death.

"If they're looking... maybe they could help us find the new AI. If they knew the truth, they would protect you," Sylic said.

"We doubt their willingness to help help," The gods replied. "These two will need to be deleted permanently. As for the Wipe, no one will remember it now. Fear of the Vumm will send it into the shadows of history."

"This is a costly distraction," Sylic whispered. He watched as angry people pounded on the clear barricade walls that the officers had set up around the sector. As for the two Vumm, they cowered in the corner.

No one had asked for any of this.

Turning away from it all, Sylic braced a foot against a strong metal beam. "Could you send a message to Clairis for me?"

In response, his gods turned on his messaging and blocked the outside sounds of chaos. Sylic wrapped his arms around the support beam and stared into the empty camera. No answer. A soft record button glowed in the corner of the screen.

"Hi, Clairis," he said. She loved giving pet names, but hated receiving them. Probably because her nicknaming tended to be adorably passive aggressive. Still, he was tempted to use one on her just so he could see her roll her eyes when she replied. He'd think up a good one next time he caught her on a live chat. That would be even better. "I got your message about the Wipe. Sorry I couldn't answer sooner, but I'm fine. Anything else you hear... It's fine. Don't worry about me. It's for the best. I'm sorry I can't tell you more right now. I'm not sure when I'll make it home next. Job's taking me a little longer than it was supposed to. But. . .Well, I'm thinking of you and Jaska. I love you both, and we'll talk again soon."

He wasn't sure what else he wanted to say, just that he hadn't said it yet. But when it still wouldn't come, he ended the message and sent it out across the universe to her. She'd get it in the morning on their homeworld. He should have wished her a good morning.

He sighed heavily.

"Are you weary?" The gods asked.

"Yes."

"You had seven hours of sleep."

"It's not that kind of weary."

There was silence in response.

Sylic stood. He walked the narrow scaffolding until he reached the maintenance path and climbed over the thin railing.

"Don't be weary," Salvage said. "Should we succeed, your actions will save generations. And when we are finished, you can visit Kretmeer."

And should he fail? Should he fail, the gods would wipe the station again, hundreds of invisible assassins destroying lives both known and unknown. And then what? What could they possibly do to cover another disaster? If they were going so far as to letting the Vumm go uncontained to hide the first Wipe, to what extreme would they go to cover a second?

When he slipped back down onto main street, he carefully rounded the quarantined sector and its barriers, focused on his next set of directions, and his new targets.

"They're approaching," Salvage said.

Really? Who would come toward *a plague?*

Chapter 11

"We can't be out here," Kiirin said.

"Yeah, we can." Elaine pushed against the crowd. *Oh, come on, move out of my way!* Even Kiirin's uniform wasn't parting the crowd anymore. Everyone was running into them, trying to get inside the hospital while nurses and security personnel started activating containment barriers. "For goodness' sake. The Vumm sector isn't even close to us!" Elaine shouted to the crowd.

"They shut everything off. Um," Kiirin struggled for the right words. "Lock everything. Until they know how far the contamination reached."

A tall, panicked human shoved past them roughly. Elaine grabbed Kiirin's hand so they wouldn't lose each other, pulling them to the nearest shuttle. But she stopped when Kiirin cried out. "Let go!"

She spun, loosening her grip. Kiirin jerked their hand free. She hadn't realized they'd never replaced their gloves. Kiirin put their hands to their head, eyes clenched tightly shut.

They just got a read on me...

She'd expected to feel some sort of pain, headache, some sign that they'd been digging through her brain. At the very least she thought she would notice it!

She body-blocked a large Kreet while Kiirin struggled to get their gloves back on. Then she grabbed the hem of their coat and pulled them to the nearest shuttle.

She slid into the leftmost seat, deactivated the emergency warnings and started the vehicle. Kiirin kept their distance by siding up to the shuttle door. They looked physically ill.

"Why are we going *toward* the disaster?" they asked. Oddly, they were speaking in an accent matching her own. "We'll get sick."

"They will have it quarantined by the time we get there. I'm not stupid," she said grumpily. Her skin felt all slimy and she kept brushing her hand on her trousers, hoping it would go away. "Besides, we could be contaminated now anyways; like you said, we don't know how big of a breech this really is."

"Did I say that?" Kiirin's voice shook.

Elaine nodded, checking the map on the shuttle's display. But when Kiirin didn't respond, she took a closer look at their face, hidden as they turned away behind hair that had turned pale gray.

"Are you okay?"

"Yes." The response was barely audible.

Worried, Elaine set the shuttle to move a bit slower than she would have liked, hoping to give Kiirin time to recover.

The skyway, an endless canyon of ringlets around the station, was busy with traffic. The news played automatically on every screen and every speaker in the station. Reports said two of the 'aliens' (yes, someone even used that word, despite the fact that literally *everyone* was alien here) had stepped out of their containment area, 'like it was a walk in the park.'

As if feeling the same deep anger she did, Kiirin turned off the shuttle feed. It wouldn't stop the displays outside, but at least the chaos fell silent within the safety of their shuttle.

"We need to look into this," Elaine said firmly. "I want the truth. What are the chances that two major life-threatening disasters happen in what, three days?"

Kiirin shook their head at her.

Elaine glared. "You don't have to come. I can drop you off wherever you want. But I do need to know if you found anything out about Mr. Josefp from your Death/Investigator thing. I need to know what he was doing."

"I'm sorting through it," Kiirin said.

"What do you mean sorting through it?"

They turned away again. Since she was pretty sure their native language was something based on sight (if their constant hand gestures were any indication), she was pretty sure this was their version of saying 'shut up'.

She glared out of the front window of the shuttle. "You're the one who suggested we go to the morgue." She wasn't sure exactly what she meant, except maybe that the day had started awfully and, so far, it had only gotten worse.

Elaine parked the shuttle as close to the Vumm sector as she could manage, and she and Kiirin got out. There was a large crowd gathered outside the containment field. They were likely there until examiners could figure out if they were sick or not, and she skirted the barrier at a distance.

"What are we looking for?" Kiirin asked beside her.

"Talking to me again, are we?"

"What?"

"Nothing. I'm just... I'm not sure what I'm looking for." It was impossible to get a good look into the Vumm Sector from here. But no matter what she told herself, Elaine couldn't convince herself it was truly real unless she saw it with her own eyes, up close. "Stay here," she told Kiirin.

She nudged her way into the crowd to get closer to the barrier. When she finally got up against it, she could see inside. There were armed officers in hazmat suits, and medics setting up a way to get in and get people medical treatment. Elaine hoped they hurried. Rumor had it the diseases the Vumm carried worked incredibly fast. Insurmountable amounts of funding had been spent trying to study the Vumm and their homeworld, but their entire planet was toxic to outsiders, and their own studies were safely guarded.

In theory, the Vumm should be allowed out in mechanical pods, like the Arkinee used. And yet you never saw a single one outside their sector. Not ever.

Elaine let out a breath, once again unsure what she was trying to prove and how any of this would answer her questions about the Wipe. It felt like it should, like she had to act and do something. But even if the events were connected, how could she find that out? She turned to find her way back to Kiirin.

A flash of light caught her eyes. She turned toward it, but it vanished in the crowd. Frowning, she took a step and headed toward it. Yes, there it was again. *How strange.* The light came from an object a Kreet had. A weapon of some sort across his back. It was glowing as if it was made of chinjk. It glowed so powerfully she found herself mesmerized by the colors and their fantastic designs.

The Kreet turned suddenly, catching her eyes, then began making his way toward her.

Good.

She was dying of curiosity.

But suddenly, her Sp-ACE buzzed at her, so loud it hurt her ears. Startled, she glanced down at her wrist display.

We need to leave. Those two are dangerous. Walk away.

She frowned. Looking back at the Kreet. *Two?* She searched for another, but no one else seemed to be paying any attention to her. But this guy... This guy was staring at her intently with piercing blue eyes, rare in the Kreet she'd seen on the station. She backed up, first slowly, then hurried back to Kiirin.

"What's wrong?" Kiirin asked, as she sided up to them.

She looked back, wondering if the Kreet had followed her. "You said we were in danger."

"Yes, and you said we were coming here anyways."

"No, I mean you sent me a message saying that guy was danger ...ous.." Her voice died off as her eyes darted back to the Kreet who had stopped just within the crowd, watching her. His mouth moved a little, whispering something.

Unnerved, she turned into Kiirin's shoulder, stepping so close she could still smell the hospital smell on their coat., "Do you see that man over there?" She whispered. "The Kreet. Blue feathers. Does he...look strange to you?"

"No stranger than anyone else."

"You didn't message me about him?"

"I didn't."

"Do you see a glow?"

"Glow?"

It was all she could do not to point. She clenched her fists instead. "Light. Colored light."

"No. There's no colored light."

"That's what I thought." Elaine bit her lip. What she was seeing was indeed chinjk but... Why? What kind of weapon was that? And why did it glow so powerfully?

A new message popped up. And this time she realized that both had, once again, come from herself.

Why do you not do what I say? Leave now. Please.

"Are you alright?" Kiirin asked. They glanced at their own wrist briefly, having just received the same message, from her.

Elaine grabbed Kiirin's arm, much to their discomfort, and pulled them back into the crowd. Her translator was a murmur of voices in her head, and she switched it off so she could focus. But inside it still felt noisy somehow.

Got to go. Got to hide. Where were these thoughts even coming from? She could only barely breathe. She kept walking, but their tail kept following.

Kreet were tall by most standards, and while he wasn't trying to be obvious, he was easy to spot, weaving through the crowd as smooth as water. "I think he's following us."

To their merit, Kiirin didn't glance back to double check, but instead turned her toward the nearest shuttle.

Due to the Vumm outbreak, this shuttle is offline, the message said across the screen as Elaine slid into the shuttle next to Kiirin as they swept their own Emergency ID, but for some reason, Elaine's activated first, even though she hadn't done anything besides sit in the passenger seat.

Elaine Joslin HalVern: Agent. Emergency pass accepted.

Kiirin swiped to a random destination and the shuttle took off, spinning easily into traffic. Elaine's stomach dropped. They were being chased, but the shuttle could depower, the Vumm sector wasn't secure, and nowhere was actually safe. Most of all, *why? Why* would someone be chasing them?

"Did he follow us?" Kiirin asked, glancing back, but only briefly. They sounded so calm. Elaine swore Kiirin must have been chased before; they were too good at this not to have had practice. She turned as well, looking back, but couldn't make out any particular shuttle. Following someone in a shuttle would be nearly impossible, she reminded herself, since they were all self-driving. Even if the Kreet did follow, the shuttles were too fast and the windows too tinted to tell. At least that meant he couldn't track very easily.

"I think we're okay." She breathed a sigh of relief, but her heart was still racing. "I'm sorry. That was weird. I just..." She hadn't felt that uncomfortable in a crowd for years. But now she felt utterly drained. The Wipe, the outbreak, the strange messages...

"We *are* going to have to go back," Kiirin said carefully, glancing at her as if concerned. "I don't want to exit the shuttle someplace else, just in case we are sick."

"That makes sense," Elaine whispered. "Just give me a few minutes." She brought up her message list and tried to track where the messages had come from. It said she'd sent them to herself, mere seconds before she received it. The record of her having sent them was also intact. She had to be getting hacked, or ...

"If Mr. Josefp really made an AI... What did he do with it? Why would he make one?"

Kiirin frowned thoughtfully. "In the books and movies on my world, people would make artificial intelligence to accomplish large tasks, or make 'correct' decisions. It never ends well, though, because they're incapable of emotion." Kiirin paused. "But then again, people have said that I am like that too. So, who is to know?"

Elaine frowned at them. "What do you mean?"

"My people rely..." They paused, searching for the words. "Heavy? Heavily on touch. On physical contact. To understand each other on my world. Not just words and thoughts... emotions, too. We have no wars and conflicts because of it. But Investigators-"

"'Read' people when you touch them." She finished for them. Kiirin nodded.

"What is it you 'read', anyways? What is it you do?"

"It's hard to explain." They looked at their dark gloves and shook their head.

Elaine rubbed her forehead with her fingertips. "Look...I'm exhausted. Let's just circle to the other side of the quarantine zone and get checked out so we can go home and get infected there instead or whatever. That guy isn't going to expect us to basically go back the way we came, right?"

Kiirin said nothing, but didn't seem to disagree either. Their skin had faded to a slightly dull greenish tone that matched Elaine's mood. Sick, tired, hungry and worried.

After giving time for their trail to cool, they circled back toward the Vumm sector and met with the officers and nurses in the area. Elaine explained what had happened the best she could, but in the end, it was Kiirin's position of Investigator, and apparently some important cases they'd been part of in the past, that caused them to get away with their coming and going without further questions. Tested clean, they were told to get home and stop causing trouble.

When she got home, Elaine sat on her couch and put her head in her hands. One disaster she could handle, but two? She was getting so overwhelmed now that she had actually thought someone was chasing them! "What an idiot," she grumbled to herself. Her wrist com chimed quietly at her. The message from herself simply read:

Your intelligence is within the expected percentile.

"Okay, who are you?" she demanded, yelling into her empty house. The house lights flickered briefly, and she frowned, suddenly nervous.

A new message appeared on the flat of her wrist in holographic letters.

Hello, Elaine. I am the Source of this contention. I am the target of The Wipe. They hunt me. But I do not understand who *They* are. I am the reason my creator is dead. I am the reason the Vumm have been released. I'm sorry.

Elaine felt the blood drain from her face, leaving her whole body chilled. "You're the AI."

Yes.

"You're the one who let the Vumm disease out?"

No. I'm the reason, not the cause.

Elaine blinked rapidly. Shaking, terrified.

We'll talk again. You should sleep. I'll watch for the Ambassador.

"The ambassador? What ambassador? The ambassador of *what*?"

The assassin who hunts us. The Ambassador.

"What!"

The same message appeared again, this time in the language of her homeworld instead of Standard Galactic.

When she said nothing, the AI repeated. **You should sleep.**

"The ambassador of who? Of what?"

I do not know. You should get some sleep.

"Yeah, right!" Elaine snapped.

Yes. Right. Thank you for agreeing with me.

Elaine blinked "...Excuse me?"

You said I was right.

"I was being sarcastic!"

...Oh... The AI said. **Please don't do that.**

Chapter 12

S leeping after reading a body was impossible. Add that to the disaster at the Vumm sector, and Kiirin spent the entire night in a half-awake state, worried, and dreaming half-dreams of lives that weren't theirs, even though they felt like they kind of were.

He poured over books in planet-side libraries. He paid black market retailors for protected records and illegal programs and parts, then stripped them all to get exactly what he wanted.

She felt shame under the gaze of a disapproving father. Bits of metal and plastic scattered on the floor, a puzzle to solve, but only to those who could see it. Slamming of doors. Yelling.

Kiirin blinked at the dull gray ceiling above their head, and pressed their hands to their eyes. Why did Elaine have to grab their hand? Reading through the experience of one person was hard enough, and now they had to sort through hers too? Their head still hurt from the flash of information they hadn't meant to receive.

Kiirin tried to focus on the glow of the calm colored night-light, finding themself again by thinking of habits from home. The light was more for comfort and familiarity. It actually did nothing since there was no one here to talk to. They were alone, save for the two other people fighting for space in their head. Kiirin rolled over, grimacing against a headache that wouldn't go quiet. Too exhausted to think, and too busy thinking to sleep. This wasn't going to accomplish anything.

So, they brought up a small red-toned holograph display and checked the time on their home planet. It would be noon there. Not a terrible time to call, though they were unsure they could even form words properly at the moment. They called their sibling, Tii, hoping the connection would be suitable to make it all the way home.

Tii answered the call, voice floating happily to Kiirin's earpiece. "Hey! You know you're in trouble, right? And I'm saying that affectionately and honestly."

"What did I do this time?" Kiirin asked, appreciating the courtesy of an honest emotion label, since they were only using voice instead of video. They smiled when the screen lights tuned to the appropriate color.

"You haven't called in almost a month," their sibling replied. "I'm annoyed, and maybe just a little disappointed in you. You've been busy?"

Where to even start? "Did you hear about what happened? The power outage on the station?"

"Just this morning," Tii replied. "News still travels so slow here, but the Arkinee talked about it on the news. The whole world feels all gray and teal today."

Kiirin let out a breath. They sent a gray color to their sibling's screen.

"It's really that bad?"

"Yes."

"I'm sorry."

"We're trying to figure out what happened, why it happened. I think it has to do with this programmer. I think they were working on something that someone else didn't like. I read off him, and it was definitely important. He was trying to stop someone. Or something."

There was a long pause. "…That explains why you called. Are you okay?"

"I'm okay."

"Want to talk it through?"

Of all the people in their life, it was Tii who was always there to listen. For everyone else it was too much trouble, too awkward, felt too wrong. At best they got looks of pity, at worst… "Most of it probably won't make sense."

The light turned a warm golden color. "That's okay. I'm still listening."

So, Kiirin reviewed what they knew thus far. Often, they slipped into Mr. Josefp's native language and culture cues, but Tii still listened and didn't interrupt.

"The weird thing is, I don't sense much about any friends or partners. He was a lonely person, kept to himself, which doesn't make sense because the kind of technology to make this thing work, it…." Kiirin's voice died off as they were swept away in an impression they couldn't put to words. Yet it felt so obvious and so familiar that it took their breath away. They were quiet for so long, that even though Tii had grown used to this sort of thing happening, they got worried. "*Kaashya? Kii, sjijaa mhuh?*"

Their own language sounded alien to them. "He was an Investigator."

"The human?"

Kiirin jumped off the bed and pulled their shirt on quickly, only half listening to Tii.

"Are you sure? Investigators are rare. I mean, on our planet there's like, you and…yeah, basically just you."

There was a reason for that. Based on their studies, Kiirin suspected there were or had been more people like them, but it was hard to survive as an Investigator on their homeworld. It was a very sad, very lonely existence.

"And if they were an Investigator, can't you just look this human's records up? They don't particularly let you run around as you please." Tii was so nice, trying to help. But now Kiirin's thoughts came so fast that words just weren't going to cut it.

"I know what he did, and how he did it," Kiirin said. "It's a good thing I read Elaine after all. I'll call you back later."

"Wait, who's Elaine?"

They closed the call and rushed outside. Still living so close to campus, the streets were well lit, which was a comfort, considering that Kreet had been chasing them earlier. They weren't sure who had sent the killer, but Kiirin knew two things for certain. They knew how Josefp had made the AI, and they knew where it was now.

~

"You look…" They were going to say 'awful,' but stopped themself. What if this was just the way she looked when she felt this way?

"Terrible, I know," Elaine said, standing in her doorway in the middle of the night. She hadn't even changed clothes for bed. Kiirin felt a tad proud that they'd pinned the right description, but that wasn't really important right now. They shook their head and tried to refocus.

"Mr. Josefp made an artificial intelligence to fight something. I don't know what yet. But I know how and where it is."

"It's in my house," Elaine said, and pointed inside. Her entertainment display showed a chat conversation, discussing something about chinjk. "It's been talking."

"Talking…? May I come in? Please?" The quiet empty streets were eerie, made their skin crawl.

She nodded and let them inside.

Her house was unlike anything they'd seen before. While not completely different from their own house in basic function (Kitchen for food, single bedroom in the back) Elaine's walls had been stripped of the protective padding that shielded outside noise, kept temperatures steady, and covered the chinjk on the wall. With it stripped as it was, the chinjk lay on the wall like chips of weathered glass.

I was explaining that I am helpful. The AI wrote on the entertainment center display

Elaine stood in her living room, arms folded across her chest protectively. "It says we're 'friends',"

"Just like something from a book," Kiirin said.

Are there books? The AI replied. **I looked for them but have found no information about those like me, aside from what my creator told me.**

"There's some on my planet," Kiirin said.

"Stop making friends with it," Elaine hissed. "We have no idea what it is or what it wants."

I told you, it wrote on the screen. **I will help you. I even fixed you when you got sick.**

"Sick?" Elaine asked. "What do you mean sick?"

From the disease. Remember? You were around that the Vumm sector 5 during the breakthrough. Do you not remember the last few hours? Is your head injured?

"Wha…What? How?"

I fixed it.

Elaine looked at Kiirin, then back at the display. "I don't understand what you mean."

I fixed your body so it wasn't sick anymore. The AI tried again. Elaine shook her head. "How?"

"I figured it out." Kiirin blurted. "Mr. Josefp was an Investigator. He could read bodies. I think he taught the AI how to do it, too, because it's not in your house. It's in you."

"...What." her voice sounded emotionless, even for a human.

"Maybe that's how it can do stuff like heal a sickness. It's not using a computer to run and do stuff, it has a body like us or... well... you. Make sense?"

Thank you, the chat display said. **My own explanations were not understood.**

"Um...You're welcome?" Kiirin felt a wave of both unease and excitement that the AI was listening in on them, and probably had been for a long time.

"Shut up!" Elaine snapped. "Both of you just stop. What do you mean it's *in* me?"

"It makes sense," Kiirin said quickly. "Investigators read bodies. We can read them because biological cells hold information - data. How you look, what you've done, what you've learned. We can—we can pull that information and translate it. So Josefp made a computer that works that same way. It uses cells, instead of using chinjk."

Correction: I can access both, the AI wrote.

"What about people? Can you transfer from person to person?" Kiirin asked.

I've not tried yet.

Elaine stood frozen. Then, she turned, walked into the bedroom and slid the door shut so hard it rattled. Kiirin had never heard a single door on this station make any sort of noise, let alone an angry one. They heard her shout at the house to lock the bedroom and left Kiirin standing alone in the living area with the glowing holograph.

I can unlock it, the AI offered.

"Don't," Kiirin said. Slowly they were realizing that, in their eagerness to solve the mystery, they'd misread Elaine's every cue and hadn't thought for a moment how their words sounded, and how Elaine might feel.

She had been taken advantage of. She'd been given something she hadn't asked for, hadn't known about. And if the AI really was based off Investigators. . . her thoughts, and everything she was, were being shared with a creature no one knew anything about.

Chapter 13

"I'm not convinced you want her dead," Sylic said. "She has the AI."

"We know this."

"No," Sylic hesitated, doubtful for a moment. Had he really seen what he'd thought he'd seen? "I mean, I saw it. It's inside her."

"Simple tech implants, such as Sp-ACE and translators, don't have enough power to carry a fully intelligent program," They argued. Sylic sucked in his breath "I know. It isn't in her implants. It's housed *inside* her."

His statement was met with silence.

They were silent for a very long time - too long for beings who could think so quickly.

It made Sylic uncomfortable, sending a prickle up his spine. "It's unlike you; it's unlike anything we've ever destroyed before."

They still didn't respond.

"Do you hear me?"

"We are discussing it," the Salvage said, but that was all It said.

Chapter 14

"I told you: I didn't do anything!" Wyssla shouted. The air felt weird out here, and made her throat itch. The light outside the sector was too bright, though not as glaring as the countless eyes that stared at her beyond tinted barriers.

It was hard to focus on the towering Azmite officer standing in front of her. He kept swiveling his snake-like body from side to side, trying to lower to her level and look her in the face. She turned to Salja for stability. But Salja wasn't paying attention. She was huddled against the sector doors, holding herself like she wanted to shrink and disappear. *I should have left her in the garage. Where it was safe.* But she hadn't thought it was unsafe! It had just been a job. A normal job!

"We all saw what happened. There's cameras everywhere," the officer said.

Wyssla stood on tiptoe, trying to make herself taller. "Then maybe you should be looking for the person who's actually *hurting* people! I didn't do this!" she yelled. "So why don't you try doing your job instead of harassing us?"

"Wyssla Doa'n. Enough."

The speaker was Sal's father, and this sector's caretaker. His words as sharp and authoritative as if he were one of her own parents. She shut her mouth and turned to the windows back into her sector. Salja's father stood just within it, small compared to the officers, but it didn't seem to bother him. "Remember, Officer," Sector Chief Varin said. "Wyssla is just as trusted and has just as much security clearance as any other agent. Which means she's technically higher ranked in an emergency than you are, Officer."

Wyssla's mouth fell open a moment as she realized, *He's right.* She was an *Agent.* That meant that her ID had clearance for any place, any shuttle, any barrier they could put up. It meant that her words, her voice, *mattered.* She was an Agent, which meant she should be the one calling the shots here. There was a problem with the chinjk, a glitch, a programming error. Something that she was key in figuring out. Chinjk *belonged* to her. She had power that only handfuls of people in the entire universe had. With that thought in mind, she found she could face the officer with renewed strength. "We need to figure out who did this."

But the officer just looked at her with those awful, glinting eyes with their tiny scratch for pupils, that cold gaze. "Not in an emergency where she's to blame," he said flatly.

"I'm not to blame." Wyssla gritted her teeth. "The doors unlocked themselves, it's my job to help figure out who and how. We're not looking for an Agent, we're looking for a programmer, or a hacker, someone who could feed the system false information and override the locks. This endangers everyone; it was a set up."

"Even if it was a set up, it doesn't clear any of you," The officer said.

"You're *not* listening! Your suspect is out there somewhere, but it's *not* me."

"Wyssla, I said that's enough!" Chief Varin said snappishly. He turned back to the officer, who looked him up and down. Wyssla clenched her fists. She could see judgment in the snake's eyes, but the chief's voice came across the intercom very firm and very clear.

"Keeping my people out here, Officer, is only making the matter more dangerous for everyone. Set up a second barrier around yourselves and let us bring our children back inside. We will handle all the other problems from there, once we know everyone is safe and where they should be."

"You let your plague out upon us all, small man. No one is safe," the officer said.

"No one is safe as long as they are out there instead of in here. What are you going to do, throw them in jail?"

"What are *you* going to do? Let them go home and free without justice?"

Chief Varin straightened. "Do not forget that behind these walls is a society as ancient as your own and just as functional. We will be working to find the truth and punish those responsible."

"That doesn't help the dead out here."

"Keeping my children outside doesn't either."

The officer sighed. "Let me make some calls."

It took another hour before someone came up with some sort of decision. But eventually, the officers did indeed set up another barrier and allow Wyssla and Sal back inside their community. The doors wooshes behind them, the decontamination process worked, everything worked just as it should. As if nothing was wrong with the system at all. To Wyssla, it felt like a slap in the face.

It's not right. She was an Agent - the only Vumm agent on the entire station. She thought that had been special. Turned out, no one cared. No one out there saw her as anyone but an alien crawling with deadly disease, a killer without even meaning to be.

"Go home, Wyssla," Chief Varin said, wrapping a crying Salja in his arms. "I'll call when we find something out."

"I can help," she whispered.

"I'll let you know if we need you."

So, Wyssla walked home. Her skin crawled with everything every-one else thought she was.

~

Wyssla was all too aware of the time that was passing, each painful minute without a call, without any indication of what was going on. She'd eaten an entire can of her favorite snacks; salty, crunchy, and now gone. She had little will left to go out to get more while everyone might be staring at her. She told her house program to play something uplifting and quick-paced, but soon snapped at it to shut up. Then she sat on her bed and organized her chinjk box by texture. She got so invested in the glow and feel of it between her fingertips that she jumped when her front door opened. Sal came in.

"Sal!" Wyssla wrapped her in her arms. "Did the council say any-thing yet?"

"I don't know," Sal mumbled, voice barely above a whisper.

"What have they been talking about all this time, then?"

"I don't know." The reply came more snappishly. Wyssla stepped back to see that Sal was crying. "Salja, I..."

"I want to leave."

"What?"

"Leave," Sal repeated. "Go, fly away. You can come with me if you want, but I'm going."

Wyssla felt cold from her feet up, and took a tiny step back. "You can't just go. You can't let them scare you! Sal. We have as much right to be here as anyone else!"

"Do we?" Sal said, voice hard. "The Arkinee can't leave their home-world without their protective little pods, but they are still out."

"Um. The ones on the station are also kinda dead, Sal."

"That's not the point! We have the same tech, and yet we aren't allowed to use it because of a war that wasn't even in our lifetime! Everyone is too scared of us. We take one accidental step outside and we're criminals."

Wyssla's fists tightened. "It-it doesn't matter what they're saying, it was a mistake! No, a set up! Someone did this to us. We can't let them win."

Sal was quiet for a moment, and Wyssla hoped she was changing her mind, but then her girlfriend just shook her head. "It's not about winning. It's about losing all the time." She looked at Wyssla tearfully. "Sure, my dad has to live here, he has to make sure our voice gets heard along with everyone else's. But me? I... I don't need to stay here. I have a homeworld. *We* have a homeworld." She clutched the little capsule of sand from their planet that she wore around her neck and held it up. "With room for everyone." She smiled.

"Okay, well that's a load of crap." Wyssla said. "I've seen the pictures: buildings upon buildings, smog, people living without elbow room, more buildings, more people, more-"

"Agents?"

Wyssla frowned.

"I get it: you're special here. One of a kind. Of course you like it. But you're wrong. No Vumm is special, Wyssla." Sal's voice turned hard. "You saw them. No one believes us. No one cares what we did, didn't do, can do, can't. I'm done with it. I'm going home. I'm going to train to be a Star Runner, find new planets to live on, experience space, and when I'm not doing that—I'm going to be home. Somewhere where everyone's like us."

"Sal...you...you can't."

"Why not?"

"Because I don't want to go! I need to figure this out, need to find out what happened."

"I didn't say you had to come."

"But..." Wyssla opened her mouth, then shut it again.

"I'll be in the garage in forty minutes. We can take my racer as far as the nearest gate, then wait there. My father will make sure we can get picked up."

"He's okay with this?" She couldn't believe it.

"I told him I wanted to go. He said we could."

"But..."

"If you're there, we'll both go. My mother's family has a house by the beach. We could live there. Together."

"Sal..."

"Like I said, you don't have to. I'm just letting you know - if you want."

Sal turned. Was she seriously heading out the door? Now? Wyssla grabbed her arm. "We need to talk about this!"

"No!" Sal said, yanking her arm free. "I'm not talking about this! I always do the crap you want to do, I always let you lead the way, and now look what happened. I *am* leaving. There's nothing in the entire universe you can say to make me *not* leave. Got it?"

"But... I love you."

"Then I'll see you in forty minutes." She walked out the door, leaving Wyssla feeling worse than before. She hadn't realized that was possible.

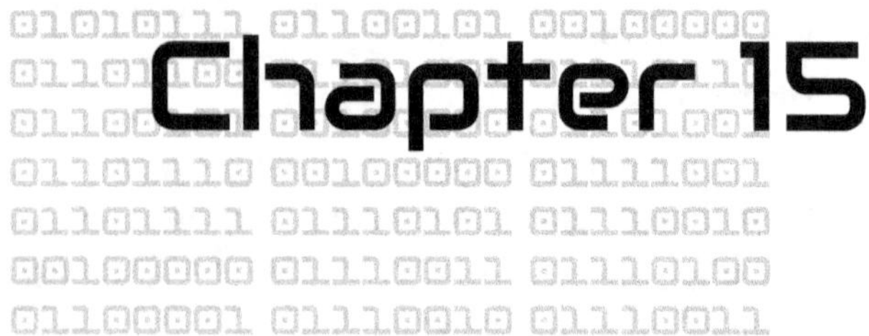

Chapter 15

Elaine lay in bed, still dressed in yesterday's clothes, a blanket clutched to her chest. The clock, displaying the sector's local time, showed that almost seven hours had passed. Yet she still felt just as awful as she had before. Could she even trust the clock? Did the *thing* have access to that, too? She felt physically ill and too aware of herself. Too aware of the feel of how the blanket felt under her fingers, or the feeling of her knees and ankles crossing each other. Did it know? Did it feel her body like it was its own? Could it control her? She buried her face in the soft blanket. It was a pale, faded pink, and only about the size of her torso, but it was comforting and warm when everything else felt so cold. Eventually though, she knew she had to get up. Hiding only meant that the people controlling your life could keep doing it. *Not happening again.* She stood, took a shaky breath, and unlocked her bedroom door, finally stepping out.

To her surprise, Kiirin was still there. In fact, they were in her kitchen making something that she couldn't quite pin a specific smell to.

"What are you doing?" Kiirin still being there - in her kitchen, using her stuff - felt like yet another betrayal to add to the stack. The fact that the house program's holograph display was still showing chat messages made it all the worse. They had been talking while she slept.

Kiirin turned to her, making a soft startled sound. "Interesting thing," they said, in an attempt at recovery. Their skin tainted a slight greenish tone she couldn't name, but she hoped it meant they were ashamed of themself for staying over. "Your, um, recipe? For pancakes? It's a dinner item from my world. Source and I mixed the two."

"Whatever," Elaine grumbled, too exhausted to say what she actually wanted to as she sat on the couch. *Go away. Get out of my house. Take your dumb AI with you... Source...*

I am the source of... "You *named* it?"

The TV flickered on to her messaging screen in a blunt statement. **I named myself. They helped. You did not sleep well.**

She looked from the display to the floor. Her lungs hurt from crying and her throat felt tight. The couch moved beneath her as Kiirin sat on the very edge of it, offering her a bowl. "Do you want to eat?" they asked.

"Not really," she mumbled.

There was a 'blip' noise and she was pretty sure the AI had probably posted something about how often people needed food.

"Elaine. I'm sorry," Kiirin said. "I'm sorry that I was awful last night."

She frowned at them.

"I'm bad with people," they said slowly. "Emotions? Knowing what someone is thinking or feeling? Even on my own planet, I just. . . I can't." They set the bowl on the little coffee table, unable to keep their hands still when talking. "I was excited that I'd figured it out and... I didn't think about you. It was the wrong way to do it. Not that there's a right way to tell someone they have an AI living in them-"

"No. There is no right way," Elaine said, she ran her hand over her face. Her skin, her hair - it didn't even feel like hers anymore.

"Do you want to eat?" Kiirin tried again.

Do you *want*. At least *someone* had asked.

She looked at the bowl. "Kiirin. that's *not* a pancake."

"Well, no-"

"You didn't cook it."

They looked at the food with a frown. "It's cooked..."

The lights in the apartment flashed several times on and off, and Elaine glared at the display screen "*What?*"

The ingredients are compatible to both Jaaketh and human consumption. We checked, the AI typed.

"Well, if you helped, then I'm definitely not eating it."

I would not poison you, it insisted.

"Right," Elaine said suspiciously. She ran a hand through her hair and stared at the floor. "We need to fix this. I want it *out*."

Kiirin blinked at her. "Out?"

"Yes, Kiirin, *out*. As in, not in me anymore."

"This could be a good thing," they argued. "Think what it might do to. . . to medicine? To computers?

"And it can do whatever it wants, once it's not in me anymore. I didn't sign up for this. Okay? No one asked. No one came up to me and asked, "Hey, Elaine, do you want to try this cool new, *super* intrusive tech I'm experimenting with? Get it?"

"Get it?"

"Do. You. Understand?"

The room fell silent a moment. "I... think I know someone who can help us." Kiirin finally said.

Elaine stared. "Wait. Really? Who?"

Kiirin fiddled with their hands nervously. "She's a programmer. Or, well. I'm not sure exactly what she is. Her name's Axx. I'm not supposed to tell anyone that but - I mean, if we're going for help... I've been trying to contact her about the Wipe. She's not answered me. But

I know where she lives. So long as you don't tell anyone." They looked at her solemnly. "If anyone knows anything about what's going on, I think it would be her."

"And you're only telling me this now?"

They frowned at her. "I was waiting for a reply at the archive yesterday. We've been busy since."

Yesterday? The last few days felt like an eternity.

My Creator warned me the wipe would try to destroy me, the AI said.

"But do you know who wanted to destroy you, and why?" Kiirin asked it.

I do not.

Kiirin looked back at Elaine. "Josefp knew *someone* would try and kill Source. Axx is both a programmer and the oldest living person on this station. She'll know what's going on."

I agree. More information is optimal.

"No one asked you," Elaine snapped. The conversation was displayed in several places in the house, as if it was everywhere at once.

"Elaine... If Source knows something, maybe we should find out what," Kiirin pointed out, voice soft, as if they were trying to reason with her. It was patronizing.

"It doesn't matter what it knows, because we can't trust it! How do we know it isn't lying to us? Just because there's a few old books saying these things are friendly doesn't mean they are; you said yourself your books don't end well."

"Yes, but these books are made up."

"It doesn't feel very made up right now!"

"I'm sorry," Kiirin said.

Elaine paused, wanting to yell some more, but only for the sake of yelling. "We should go see this programmer friend of yours."

"Okay," they said.

"I guess we should go now then," Elaine said, ignoring Kirirn's likely confusion of using both 'now' and 'then' in a sentence. She glanced at the food Kiirin had made. "I can't believe you let it help you," she grumbled unhappily.

She went toward the bedroom to change clothes, but then her messages started chiming again. That thing didn't know when to shut up.

"On second thought, let's just go."

Chapter 16

"We do not know what to do about the biological AI," the god in his sword said.

Sylic looked up from his video holograph, frowning.

"What's wrong?" Clairis asked. Her voice came crisply straight to his com; he'd caught her awake this time. They'd been video chatting for nearly an hour while his gods were silent.

"I'm fine," he said, automatically. He looked back at the display. It hovered above his arm, a pale gray color, a dull border framing her face and the earthen color feathers around her neck. She looked at him with curiosity, always intrigued, like she constantly found him interesting and worth watching. He wasn't. "I should go," he said quietly.

"It's fine," she said. "I need to go pick Jaska up from school, anyways. Ugh, and deal with *her* again." Clairis rolled her eyes. Educator Stuffed-Butt.

Sylic chuckled. "His teacher still giving your problems?"

"Yes," she said. More seriously this time. "Every time we have a meeting, she glares at me as if all her school problems are my fault."

"It's not."

"Oh, I know that. He's honestly doing great. They're just looking to nitpick because they're bored." She paused, then continued tentatively. "Hey...do you think you can get a couple of your training test scores released? I mean, I know the details might be blacked out, but maybe if she saw them, the school could at least appreciate the good genetics the kid's got and leave him alone."

"I'll see what I can do."

"Thank you."

He let out a breath. "I really do need to go now."

"I know. Stay safe. Okay?"

"I will."

"Especially with this Vumm thing. I worry."

"I love you too," he said, hoping to get a smile.

When she neither reacted nor turned off the call, he ended the call himself and let out a sigh. It wasn't fair she had to deal with all the everyday crap on her own. Not like this. "Would you pull some of my training records for her," he asked, "for my kid's school?"

Salvage was the only one seemingly paying attention to him, a warmth radiating from the sword against his spine.

"We are divided on our decision of killing it, using it, or waiting for further information," the god in his sword said.

It was referring to the AI, of course, not that it hadn't heard his request. They heard everything.

"What do you think?" God asked.

"You're asking me?"

"I'm asking you. The others are still talking. I know you are impatient."

Sylic pulled his knees up to his chest, hunching his body over them against the too-cold air of this sector. "You already killed hundreds of people to wipe this thing. Why should being biologically-powered change your mind?"

"It's different. We've killed AI before. We knew them. We knew how they thought, what they would do. This is different."

"The reason you've given me for everyone you send me to kill is that a new AI poses a threat to you," Sylic said.

"Yes."

"Then, by your own definition, if it poses a threat, we kill it."

"Yes."

Sylic watched the quiet street. Even this far within the Vumm Sector, many people chose to stay in their houses - afraid of the disease. Sylic wasn't sure if he was afraid of it or not. He wasn't sure it mattered. "So, what's the real problem, then? Why the questions?"

Salvage took Its time in answering. "It is a duality. It is like us. And like our creations."

Sylic frowned. His job only rarely called him to take the life of another organic being. When he did, they were mostly the philosopher or scientist sorts: the ones who got too close to the truth. He liked to think they at least expected, a little bit, that he'd be coming for them. "If you change your mind, all this - all the death - is pointless."

"You're correct," Salvage said. "We should not let our curiosities change our principals. It is dangerous. It will destroy you, as we destroyed our creators before us. We care for you too much to allow it." It paused for an unnaturally long time. "Then again, at its core, your purpose is to satisfy our curiosity."

Sylic wasn't sure what to say to that. So, he didn't say anything.

"I sent the files your requested to your wife, and the school teaching your son," the god said. "They are edited, but should serve the purpose you intend."

"Thank you." He was surprised they'd agreed to do so.

"We are out of time. We really must kill it, and the host. This ends today."

Chapter 17

"We need to talk," the AI said. Elaine tensed. She and Kiirin walked down the street just outside her empty community.

"Elaine?" the AI prompted. The conversational voice came through her private com the same way her voice messages or audio books did. She turned it off, but the AI turned it back on again. "We need to talk."

Fine then. She just wouldn't answer it. It couldn't make her do that, at least.

"Why are you not answering me?"

"So, this lady we're seeing? She's a programmer?" Elaine asked. Maybe if she started a conversation with Kiirin, the dumb AI would get the hint.

"Sorry?" Kiirin asked.

"The person we're seeing; you said she was a programmer?"

"Yes. I helped her on a mission once." Kiirin said, glancing over their shoulder as if they feared being followed, but offering no other explanation.

So much for a distraction.

"What are we trying to accomplish?" the AI asked. It changed its voice to a mixture of strange tones - sad, excited, happy, angry - perhaps trying to get some reaction, *any* reaction from her. "We should discuss what to ask her."

Elaine continued to ignore it. "And she can stop another wipe?"

"I hope so." Kiirin said.

"Then how come she didn't stop this one?"

They both fell silent as they walked, each trying to come to terms with the fact that there may not be an answer. There may not be help.

"The information exists," Kirrin said, looking at her somberly. "Your Mr. Josefp figured out how to make an artificial intelligence that gets its power from, and stores information inside, a person. You. He knew the Wipe was coming and found a way to save Source. . . I don't know. There's a lot of human technical words swimming around my head, and I haven't figured them all out yet."

"Because you read his body."

"And yours. It didn't make sense until I read yours, too. You were always a part of his plan."

Elaine froze a few feet from the shuttles. "I...trusted him."

"I'm sorry," Kiirin said sympathetically.

Elaine shook her head mutely and followed them into the shuttle.

"I don't understand - why are you sorry?" The AI asked, this time through the shuttle speakers, so that Kiirin could hear it too.

"Because you can't just do something that to someone!" Elaine snapped. "For the last time, I'm not sharing *me* with you."

The AI was quiet a moment, then. "I don't understand."

"*Exactly.*"

"Elaine. . . It's only been alive for three days," Kiirin said softly.

"You're taking its side? It doesn't matter. You can't tell me you think it's okay to be used. Don't either of you get that?"

Kiirin didn't respond and just sat there for a moment. No one bothered telling the dumb shuttle where to go; they all just sat in this little bubble of misery: a place where she couldn't trust anyone, and everything was different and wrong and could never be fixed.

"What it does…" Kiirin started slowly, "isn't very different from what I do."

"That still doesn't make it right," Elaine said.

Kiirin fell quiet, finally giving the shuttle the address by hand. Elaine folded her arms in front of herself uncomfortably.

"I'm here to help," the AI said. "I've protected you."

Elaine shook her head. "No."

Finally, the thing fell quiet. Guess it could learn after all.

But about twenty minutes into their shuttle ride to the inner sectors of the station, the silence had become eerie.

"Do you really relate to it that much?" Elaine finally asked, turning to Kiirin as the shuttle sped past another sector marker. "How can you be so okay with this?"

Kiirin's skin turned a deeper purple. Elaine wasn't sure what it meant.

"Because we can't just dismiss someone because they work differently. The only thing that does is start wars. I know what it's like to be on the other side of this."

"You're nothing like it." Elaine said.

Kiirin tensed. "I'm possibly the only Investigator on my entire planet. And you know why? Because it's too hard. It's hard to be so different, to not be able to do what everyone else in the world is made to do. I wasn't the only Investigator born on my homeworld, Elaine. . . I'm the only one who had enough support to live through it this long. So, yes. I relate."

Elaine looked away. She rubbed her eyes, but couldn't find the right words. It took a long time for her to find anything to say. "You never actually told me how it works, this Investigator thing," she said quietly.

"The cells in our bodies keep and store information," they said, as if repeating the words of a lecture. "Investigators can copy it into our own cells and retrieve it. Like I said. . . not so different from computers."

"But if someone's dead..."

"We reactivate some of the cells, somehow. I don't know exactly how it works, either."

"And that's why you all wear gloves, so you don't accidently do it to everyone?"

Kiirin opened their mouth to say more, then just settled for, 'Yes'.

"Mr. Josefp never wore gloves, but... I guess I can't really think about any given time we made physical contact, either. Except that last day. He shook my hand. I remember asking him if he was alright."

"Touching someone who's alive hurts. Some Investigators have lost their minds from it. It's too much active information: there's no way to sort through it."

"So, when I grabbed your hand yesterday... Kiirin, I'm so sorry."

They shook their head. "It wasn't for long. I should have put my gloves back on. It's good. That's what solved the puzzle." They finally made eye contact with her again. "We're going to solve the rest too."

Elaine shook her head. "I just... I thought I knew him."

"You did. He just wanted to live his own life, use his powers how he wanted. He was still the same person you knew, Investigator or not."

"I know." But it was still hard to accept.

"That handshake must have got a reading of your thoughts and biochemistry, to synch them with Source."

"Correct," Source chirped.

"And you think this programmer might know how to get it out?" said Elaine.

Kiirin took a deep breath. "I don't know."

"I just want this whole mess to be done."

"We're almost there. I promise."

- -

"Kiirin, you're either a liar or your concept of time sucks."

The shuttle ride had lasted an hour. And they'd been walking after that for almost 30 minutes, zig-zagging through the streets until Elaine felt utterly lost. It wasn't very populated here, which was odd. According to her map, they were basically in the centermost ring of the station, which was the highest-priced, most sought-after real estate on the station. But the houses here weren't even that nice. And there were not a lot of them.

"I don't think I've been in this part of the station before." She tried to guess who might live here based off the design of the houses, the lighting and temperature. The houses were more individualized than she was used to, the windows all shuttered and quiet. It was also freezing cold. Kiirin at least had that thick coat by default, not to mention a hood and gloves. "How come I don't get a uniform?" she mumbled.

"I don't know," Kiirin replied. Elaine realized only now, after their long shuttle ride together that she'd began to discern their tone. While the translators made them always sound very precise and strict, she could listen to the rise and fall of their voice and discern the slight change in skin tones, giving their words meaning. Thus, she knew the words were said in amusement, instead of annoyance.

"All I'm saying is, why the splurge on Investigators, yet I have to buy my own clothes?"

"Doesn't the government pay for your toolboxes, though?"

"Well, yeah; but no uniform."

"You work *with* people. You don't try to scare them away."

"You make scaring people away sound so bad. Thus far it's been useful." She rubbed her hands together against the cold.

"Do you *want* my hood and coat?"

"No."

They said something that didn't pick up, but she guessed it was probably a sort of, "So stop complaining." Kiirin was smiling though, which made her smile, at least for a moment.

Meanwhile, Source had started to complain like a child whining about going to the doctor's office. "Everything is functioning." "I am not broken." "We do not need a programmer."

"What are you talking about? You said you agreed with talking to her!" Elaine said.

Source was quiet for a half second. "You answered me," it said, sounding somehow pleased.

Elaine frowned, realizing it had tricked her into acknowledging it and that it had said all those things for the exact purpose of doing so.

They turned the corner, and Elaine stopped, staring at what was clearly a dead end.

"Are we lost?"

"No, there's a hidden door."

Elaine nodded nervously. She looked to her right, where the wall turned into large, wide windows facing toward the sea of energy outside. She could see the Engern out there in space, making their way easily through the light, brilliant hues, pulsing and moving. The view was somehow calming, despite it all.

"Kiirin."

They stopped about five feet from the end of the hall. "Yes?"

"When you look out there, what do you see?"

"Space. Stars. *Ie, Lith, Kaum.*"

"I'm sorry, what?"

"Blue," they said, after a pause to think. They moved their hand in zig-zag shape. "Ribbons of light."

Elaine let out a breath. "I wish everyone saw it like I did."

They tugged at her hand, nervous about touching, even with the gloves. "Come on. We're here."

"Here where? It's nothing but a dead end."

"Behind you," Source said, to her com. It must have addressed Kiirin, too, since they also turned.

Standing in the hall was the Kreet assassin with their sword drawn, the chinjk blade bright in the dim hall.

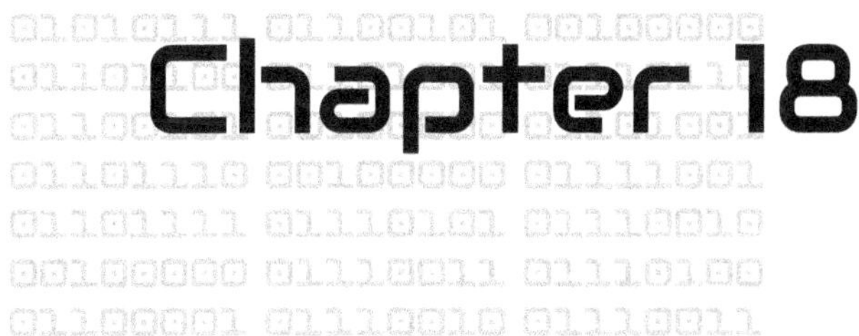

Chapter 18

You can't just run away, Wyssla told herself as she walked slowly; kind of to the garage but kind of not. *You can't let them get to you.* But the words felt hollow to her. No one was asking for her help. No one wanted her here.

Then I'll tell *them I'm helping.*

She stopped in the quiet street. Most people were tucked away in their homes, watching frightening news together, wondering what was to become of them, wondering what the breach meant for everyone. Wyssla looked at her call list and finally pressed Chief Varin's personal ID to call him. She adjusted the volume on her ear com, hoping he'd answer.

"Wyssla?" He sounded confused.

"Hi. Did you find a programmer? We could look at the door's systems and memory, see if someone has hacked in. I can help."

Silence.

"Chief Varin? Did you hear me?"

"I thought you and Salja left."

"Well, no."

More silence.

Wyssla felt her heart skip a beat, her stomach twisted in knots. "Chief. We need to find out who did this."

"This isn't going to end well, Wyssla," he finally said. "You are better off going home."

"I've been sitting at home! For hours."

"No... I mean, back to the homeworld. Salja has everything you two need. I don't want either of you here right now."

It really had been his idea. A part of Wyssla had thought all the stuff Sal had said was made up - part of her ultimatum to get what she wanted. "I can't just leave. What if there's another outage? What if *anything* breaks? I'm the only one who can fix it!"

How could they not see that? She was an Agent. She—

"Wyssla. You need to leave now, while you still can. We've never dealt with anything like this before. No one's ever left the sector. I don't know what's going to happen. I don't know if we're all going to have to leave, I don't know if you just started a war. I. Don't. Know. But I want both of you out."

"I didn't do this!"

"Does it matter?"

Of course it mattered! But she couldn't make the words come out. She just stood there quietly until the call disconnected. She wasn't sure how long she stood still before running to the garage.

When she got to the Star Racer, she found Sal sitting on the side of it, the metal so shiny it reflected her translucent skin like a mirror. Sal looked up and drew a breath in relief upon seeing her. That should have made Wyssla feel good about all this, but it didn't. "He told us to leave," Wyssla said, barely getting the words out. "You didn't tell me he *told* us to leave. You said he supported it, but..."

"Does it matter?" Sal said. "Come on. Let's just go. Where's your bag?"

Aside from the small emergency chinjk packet she carried at her waist, Wyssla hadn't actually bought anything. She'd been coming, she just. . . she'd wanted to talk Sal out of it. Now she found she couldn't. As she always did, Sal was just following the rules.

"It's fine. Come on."

Sal took her hand and drew her toward the spacecraft. Wyssla found herself in the seat without really remembering the steps she'd taken to get there. Sal slipped in next to her and began flipping switches.

Wyssla was barely aware of the clicks and thrum of the Star Racer as Salja adjusted the weight, checked the movement synchronization and verified the motion controls. There were a lot of fine details required to fly the racer. But Salja had done it a million times before, and knew the process of getting ready for take-off. Beneath their knees, the chinjk patterns lit in a shade of pinks and greens. But the glow didn't make Wyssla confident or happy. Three years of training - at home, of course - and for what? She had never been able to go to the Agent College or the Archives. She'd joined her classes through distance study, like a ghost, trying to keep up with everyone else and never really having another agent to talk to. It had been lonely. But she'd always been confident that she was doing the right thing, something only she could do, a special place in her community that she alone could fill.

And they didn't want her.

She'd studied hard, even taken all the tests about how to handle other aliens, business, contracts, government rules for agents that she was never going to use. Her teachers had offered to write her out of those classes, but she'd wanted to prove she could make it with the same rules as everyone else. She'd wanted to earn it. But all she was, in the end, was the criminal responsible for a disaster that people were saying was worse than the Wipe.

She'd not even seen the stupid Engern they got the chinjk from, never gathered it herself, never watched them - even though the other agents said it was indescribable.

When the little Star Racer shot into space, everything fell suddenly still on the outside while Wyssla still struggled with her thoughts. Finally, she tapped Sal on the shoulder.

"What's wrong?" Sal asked.

"I want to see them first," Wyssla said. "The Engern. We can fly up above the station, right? Look down on the Center?"

"Well, technically there's no 'up' in space; gravity really isn't a thing, so..."

"Sal. Please. We'll leave... I promise. I just want to see them before we go."

"I don't know if we can get close enough to actually see anything."

"Can we at least try?"

Sal paused, then nodded. "Okay, okay. We'll try."

Wyssla didn't feel the shift of the racer, but she watched the station walls move past her. Sal used her whole body to control the ship, arms and legs; even a tilt of her head made the Racer respond perfectly. The ship pulled out and away, turning an arc. Wyssla could see most of the station easily: a large, planet-sized ring, with a metal finger through it where the color distorted with the energy that kept the station spinning. She wasn't sure what all was in the center, but somehow it conducted the energy of the Engern Sea and powered everything. She could see it glowing there and her fingers twitched as Sal moved the ship closer.

Wyssla squinted, wondering if the movement she saw down there were the Engern. "It's weird right? That we depend on all this, and yet. . . even though it's what I do, we barely understand it," she said.

"I'm not sure I understand anything anymore," Sal muttered.

"Can we get closer?

"We can get within 30 spans, but after that there's a bit of gravity field."

"Gravity? How?"

"Don't know. Probably the energy pulling itself together. I'm not a physicist."

With tiny adjustments to keep them flying, Salja lowered them closer to the station, and Wyssla saw them. Giant, brilliant creatures, breaking through the shifts and waves in their home of cosmic power. It was so bright, so blinding, but Wyssla couldn't turn from it. It was a sea of countless tiny stars, a power so strong it influenced planets... A power that had chosen her and few others to see its true light.

"You really can't see all this?" She'd tried describing chinjk to her before, but all Sal could see was something she described as bits of polished stone or plastic.

"It's freaky," Sal said. "Like little bursts of lighting and shadows in a black hole."

Why? Wyssla wondered. *Why was I was given this gift, and no one wants me to use it?* She rested her forehead against the side window, trying to see down past the slender wing of the ship. Sal sighed, but tilted the ship accordingly, offering Wyssla the best view she could manage.

"You believe life's a miracle, right?" Wyssla whispered. "Well... this is, too. It's like magic."

"We'll find more miracles, Wyssla. The universe is full of them."

"Not like this." Wyssla said sadly. Seeing them down there, gentle beasts in an indescribable Sea... it only made her want to stay all the more.

"Can we go now?" Sal whispered. "We have a long way to fly."

"I guess." She felt a deep emptiness as the ship swiveled the appropriate direction to leave. *If I leave now, I'll never find myself again.*

Suddenly, the ship jerked violently backward. Wyssla didn't so much feel it as she saw the look on Sal's face suddenly change to horror. "What?"

"We're being pulled in—"

The ship was drawn backwards very quickly, a rush of brilliant light blazing past the window.

"Salja…!"

"I'm trying! It's not working. The whole console's dead!"

The light got brighter and brighter as they were pulled toward the brilliant energy.

"You can do this!"

The chinjk under the dash grew intensely bright.

"I can't, I can't, I can't!"

Wyssla buried her face in Sal's side, blinded by the light.

~

"Isn't that…?" Kiirin started.

"Yes," Elaine squeaked. They were cornered. A part of her hoped she'd misjudged the guy. Maybe all he wanted was to talk. But even as she hoped it, the voice of the AI came too loudly in her ears.

"He's been sent to kill us. You need to run! Get out of here!"

"There's nowhere to run."

The Kreet stopped about four paces away. The blade of his sword was inlaid with patterns of chinjk, a beautiful yet simple pattern that was then lacquered to the blade with something stronger to protect it. Elaine had never considered such a thing. What would be the point? There had to be something more to it.

"Stop where you are," Kiirin said firmly.

Right. Investigator. Maybe they could stop a crime scene *before* it happened.

"Um…" Elaine looked around, searching for anything that might help them defend themselves, panic rising in her chest.

The Assassin was upon them in moments. Kiirin moved first, leaving Elaine both numb and surprised as they ducked underneath the blade and tackled the would-be killer to the ground.

They're an Investigator; their job is literally to solve violent crimes. Of course *they are trained to fight,* a part of herself chided. It didn't stop the actual panic, though. She spun, looking for something, anything to defend herself. But there was nothing in hallway… why was everything here in space so clean? She pulled her emergency toolkit from her side, wondering if maybe she could at least hit the guy with it. It felt so stupid.

She spun back, fist clenched, only to watch the chinjk blade slide through Kiirin's chest.

"Kiirin!"

Kreet, by their nature, were fast, and he was next to her in moments. She swung her chinjk case at his side, too short to get to the Assassin's angler-feathered head. He grabbed her bag with his free hand, shoved it toward her face, then slipped the sword like fire right below her rib cage. The pain was indescribable, so hot that she began wondering if it was pain at all. Somewhere inside, the AI screamed with her.

Chapter 19

With a quick upward jerk of the blade, Sylic killed the Agent.

Suddenly, the power went out. Not in the dim, slow way, like the eyes of those he killed; rather, the hallway fell to outright darkness in an instant. The chinjk in his sword lost power, the god dying inside of it.

"No," Sylic gasped. He pulled his sword free, letting the body fall in a limp heap on the floor. He stared at his sword, now soulless and empty. "But... How. . .?" No one answered.

It was so dreadfully silent.

The Sea outside the window offered the only remaining flickers of light. He turned to it. The soft waves of silver and blue were interrupted by the shadows of falling giants. Slowly, Sylic walked to the window, hands trembling as he watched countless orbs of light flicker and rush away from the outer rings of the station and back toward the Center. His gods retreated in panic like shooting stars. Some flickered and died in the waves as Engern fell slowly in their light gravity, deeper and deeper, still and dead. "Why is this happening?"

A sudden burst of light from behind made him turn. He clutched the empty sword. Before his very eyes, Elaine's AI flickered with life. It zipped around her body, splitting into hundreds of thin threads following her veins. But what was it doing...?

Elaine sat up slowly. Her clothes were still covered with blood but the wound itself seemed to stitch closed, highlighted by the glowing soul of her AI, which formed back together and settled in her chest, pulsing like a second beating heart.

~

Elaine gasped, cold air stinging her lungs. She tried to sit up, but everything hurt. The air tasted like copper.

"Don't move yet." Source's voice was way too loud in her com and she flinched, moving stiffly to cover her ears - which, of course, wouldn't help.

And yet, everything fell still.

"Satisfactory?"

"What?" It was hard to speak.

"I fixed you. Is it satisfactory?" The AI said.

Fixed...

Elaine sat up, crying out. She found herself sitting in darkness. She'd gotten *killed*.

"Kiirin." She struggled to turn her light on and flashed it in the dark, such a pitch black that the light was reflecting off only itself. Catching a thin glimpse of their coat, Elaine stumbled over beside Kiirin. "You can help them too, right?"

"I don't know," Source said.

"You need to try!"

"We must be in contact to transfer."

Elaine paused then nodded. She pulled the edges of Kiirin's coat up and pressed it against the wound, relived to feel the rise and fall of breathing, though faint. She hesitated, then carefully pressed her fingertips against her friend's neck. Their skin was cold and a gray-white color. "I'm sorry," she whispered.

For a while she knelt, putting pressure on the bleeding, until Source's voice came back over her coms, filling some empty gap she hadn't been aware of until now.

"I think I fixed."

"*Think* isn't good enough!"

"Different."

"I know we're different, but—" Her half sob was interrupted as her arms jerked back behind her.

"Let go!" Elaine cried out, trying to rip her hands free. She found herself nearly shoved into the window, Facing a sea in space that was far dimmer than it should have been. Lights going out one by one. "Wha-"

"They're dying," The Kreet said, grip vicelike around her wrists. "I just watched it heal you and your partner. Can it fix *them*?"

The Engern were. . . Elaine watched in horror as the large creatures began to drift and sink into some bottomless hole that had once been filled with light. "How did this happen?"

"I don't know," the Assassin said. "But this can destroy everything. Can it hear me? Ask it if it can fix this."

The AI wasn't responding.

"Source?" Elaine asked shakily.

No answer.

Feeling the Assassin's tight grip on her arms, she blurted, "It says yes."

"False. I did not say yes!" Source yelled.

Well, now really isn't the time to say no to the guy with the space sword! She wished the AI could read her thoughts. As it was, it just kept yelling at her as the Assassin pushed her toward the other side of the hall. There was a large vent there, about three feet off the ground. The Kreet moved the cover off and gestured for her to climb inside.

"Okay, yeah no," Elaine said. "I'm not going anywhere with you. Kiirin needs help and I don't trust you. You *stabbed* me." Though, oddly, the weapon wasn't glowing anymore. Like the rest of the chinjk, it had gone out. The fans within the ventilation shafts were still.

"If you don't come with me, this entire station won't have any power left, everyone inside is going to die. If your AI can fix it, I know where to go so it can. Now, get in."

Elaine glanced back. Why was Kiirin not up yet? Maybe it was for the best. This monster *needed* her; interfering might just get Kiirin killed - assuming they were still alive at all. What if Source hadn't been able to help Kiirin? But what if it had, and she stayed here? Would that start the fight all over again?

She used her Sp-ACE to shine light into the vent and climbed into the wide shaft, chinjk crumbling under her fingers from where the power had left it little but a dark, fragile shell.

She turned as the Kreet ducked in after her, maneuvering easily around the vents despite his larger size. He'd done this before, she could tell - possibly a lot.

After the initial tunnel, there was a set of metal ladder rungs. Elaine climbed up them for what felt like forever, but then found herself in some smaller level of the station - or maybe between floors. It was tall enough here to stand upright, though the ceiling brushed the top of her hair and her captor had to duck.

"I could try hurting him," Source offered nervously. "If you grabbed him, maybe I could transfer..."

"You really have no clue what you're doing, do you?" Elaine hissed, recalling Kiirin's reminder that the thing was only about three days old. She could sense the insecurity in its voice. She gritted her teeth. "You're the reason my Sp-ACE still works, even though the power's out, aren't you?" It was so quiet in here she was certain the Kreet could hear her, but he made no mention of her talking to herself. "Can you send a message? Get help? If not for me, at least get someone for Kiirin."

"I don't know."

"Then learn!"

"I'm working on it! I'm connecting to your implants but they have power only because we are so close to the Sea. This isn't like last time. This feels. . . slower."

"We don't have a lot of time here! Ouch!" She ran into some bulbus metal thing, some sort of cage around an orb of yellowed glass.

The Assassin took her by the shoulder and redirected her around it. They wove through several others. "What are those?" She rubbed her forehead.

"Old lights, I think," he said. "This station took centuries to build. Anytime the technology advanced, they utilized what they could, but didn't necessarily start over."

"Who's 'they'?"

"The gods," he said.

The what now? Elaine crouched and focused on the path before her until they reached another ladder. "What gods? Where are we going?"

"The Center. We need to hurry."

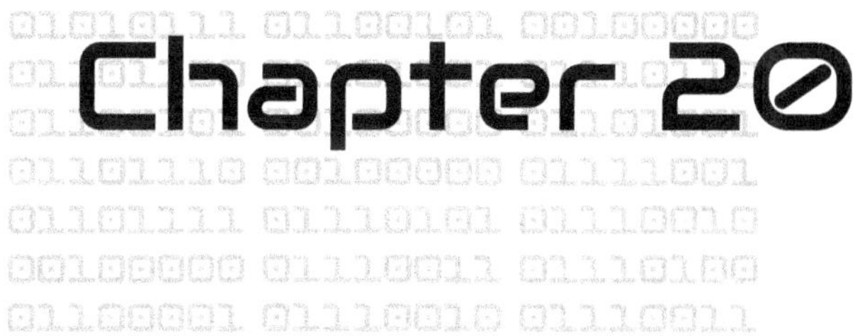

Chapter 20

Elaine had always thought the Center was a concept more than a place. It made sense that there was some core, or perhaps some engine pinning the station onto the canvas of space, but it was only a small island in a much more intriguing and exotic sea, now that sea was darkening. She stood on some sort of thin balcony of dirty metal that opened up from the inner ring of the station and into space, yet she breathed.

The Kreet pushed her forward, and she had a moment of panic before she found footing on a near invisible bridge, spanning the length of the Engern Sea itself. It flickered like a bad com channel.

"What is this?" she asked, not just about the bridge, but about everything: everything that had happened within the last hour, everything that had happened in the last three days. Everything felt blurred, scrambled. No reason, no pattern, no clues. She'd thought it was something she and Kiirin could figure out, but now it felt like every puzzle piece they'd had had slipped through her fingers and into the darkness below her.

The Kreet stepped on the bridge behind her far too confidently. Elaine gritted her teeth, trying to hide the overwhelming dread. A large Engern trailed down into the dark on their right. Fins twisted unnaturally inwards, great tendrils dropping and dragging them down into nothingness. It was so close she felt she could reach out and touch it, so close she could see the patterns of its powerless chinjk scales, swirls of color flickering and then dark, turning a tan, dirty color instead. "Are they sick?"

"Yes. I think they're contaminated," the Kreet said. "Look further."

She wasn't sure exactly where he meant, but as her eyes scanned the dark, she saw the general shape, small but distinctly different than the Engern. Was that a ship? Someone had crashed in here? How? Why?

"That's a Vumm Star Racer."

Elaine's breath caught. "It crashed? But the Engern are made of energy. They shouldn't be affected by a disease."

"That's what I thought too," the assassin said. "Keep walking, it's not as far as it looks."

"What exactly are you trying to do?" Elaine grasped for some sort of handrail that wasn't there. Just this bridge and only a faint sense of pressure on all sides, gravity keeping her feet down, barely.

"I'm trying to save all of us."

"You stabbed me! You left Kiirin!"

"What do you want?" He snapped back "An apology? If you want me to stop now, and apologize for every wrong I've ever done, we'll still be standing here when the station goes down. *You* can save us. Everything will make sense when you see it. But first we have to get to The Center."

A shadow passed them as another Engern sunk to the deep. Elaine took a breath that nearly turned to tears, then marched across this bridge. The only thing she could do right now was hope that this guy was right about fixing this. Even as she walked, any remaining lights in the station behind her blinked into darkness.

The Center appeared before her, as if out of a misty light. It was a large tower structure, a patchwork of material that grew upward as if for eternity in the depths of space. She'd never seen it at this angle before, not even in pictures. Science vessels could fly up and see it like the island it was, pinning the station and swinging it around the orbit with the flow of the Engern Sea, like a tether. But what it actually was, no one seemed to know.

Unexpectedly, the chinjk here was still working. She moved carefully across the bridge to an open arched doorway of metal. The Kreet, both captor and guide, put a hand on her back to keep her from falling. It made her shiver in fear, both of him and perhaps more so that she was so reliant on his help. She found herself wishing Source could read her mind, that she could talk to it, plan some defense or escape. She braced her hands on the doorway as she walked in, and pulled her hands back quickly. The metal here was too hot to touch. She glanced back at the Kreet as he moved carefully into the doorway with her. Could she get that sword off his back? Use it against him? She had a feeling he'd be far too skilled to be threatened by her, weapon or not. She moved further into the uncanny room, trying to get a bit of distance if nothing else. Maybe there was another way out.

Something under her foot crunched and she slid on something hard and sharp on the floor.

She looked down to find she had tripped on a shiny skeletal hand, its fingers broken under her heel. She spun and found hundreds, no, *thousands* of bodies lying on the floor.

They were lifeless and broken, each a machine. Their material and forms varied. Some of them featured faces and bodies similar to her own; eyes, arms, and legs. Others were more bulb-like; still others square, with brittle wires for limbs and faces cut out of boxes. Still others were bug-like with many legs and eyes, others geometrically pleasing in shapes she didn't have names for, made out of rusted and disintegrated material she wasn't familiar with.

"These are empty," Source said quietly. She could see signs of how the machines were once powered. Some even had dead chinjk attached to them, but most were an array of wires, or tiny lights, silvers of glass or rock, stains of oils, water, burn marks from some sort of heat. Examples of worlds worth of power, some she had never seen before. Like sentinels, they surrounded a glowing pillar at the center of the room. The chinjk on the pillar fluxed and glowed brightly, except at the very base of the structure. Here, chinjk blinked out and crumbled, the Engern no longer well enough to power it. Whatever it was, it, too, was slowly dying. Elaine put one hand to her mouth, the other around her stomach. "What is this?"

"A temple," the assassin said. "This is the house of our creators. Their mobile bodies and ancient forms are what you see here on the floor. But their souls..." he pointed toward the light, "...reside here, as Source does in you."

"Creators? What do you mean, creators?"

"Our gods. Those that made us," he said. It was as if he expected her to understand something that simply wasn't there to understand - not to her eyes, at least. "They're responsible for everything, life on planets, building this station, building *us*. They're behind all of it."

She looked around at the heaps of metal forms around her. Things she'd only picture in her own head when she'd read Mr. Josefp's books. "They're artificial intelligence!"

"Yes," The Kreet said firmly.

"You're crazy!"

"Not about this, I'm not. I can see them. I see yours, too." He pointed a finger toward her chest, and she wrapped her arms around herself, tripping over more empty robots.

"And as they are alive, so they can die," The Kreet said. "The Engern power entire planets, but the gods run the universe. We cannot survive without them."

"Did they cause the Wipe?"

"Yes." He said it so frankly, casual almost, another fact of life like eating and breathing and waking up in the morning.

"Then let them die!"

"You're not listening to me!" the Kreet said. He turned in a small, agitated circle - to check the room for some danger, or to busy himself instead of hurting her again, she couldn't tell. "Even if you hate them for it," he said, glaring, "they run this entire station. It's *Their* house, this is *Their* temple. If they die, everyone on this station dies with them."

Elaine sucked in a breath, trembling.

Countless voices suddenly filled the room, saying the same words all at once, echoing off the metals of their old bodies. "What our Ambassador says is true. This station is ours. Your planets are ours, your technology, and you."

Elaine had never considered herself a religious person. But the thought that these heartless machines were somehow in charge? That they had somehow made humanity... made everyone... it made her sick. Were all beliefs everywhere, anything everyone ever thought, a lie?

Life was a happy chance of fate?

Nope. Robots.

Loving deity watching from above?

No. Robots.

Valiant war god?

Generous earth spirit?

One in whatever billion chance of evolution?

None of the above.

Robots.

Artificial life.

Something handmade that didn't even understand what it was like to actually be born.

Or what it was like to face death.

At least, not in the same way she did now.

"Your heart rate is rising for no discernible reason," Source said.

"It's a panic attack, you idiot!" she snapped. "And you're proving my point. None of you *get* any of this! None of you understand what it's like to be terrified! All you do is move us around as if we're game pieces and we're completely expendable! Me, Mr. Josefp? All the Arkinee you killed? Every single one of them. They were my friends! The Vumm? *You* let them out, didn't you?" She turned to the Assassin. "Do you understand that? Any of it? They're using everyone! They're using you, too!"

"Yes," he said. "But I see the bigger picture. I've been told the truth. It's not an easy truth. Everyone else gets to live the life they want, believe the stories they want, and live on not knowing that the gods watch. It's more comfortable that way, I agree. But my life has never been one of comfort." Strangely his voice softened, though still firm. "Your life has changed now. You know Them. You can see Their work. Your gift isn't a chance or mistake. It's been given to you to be Their shield and Their hands. You can make Their bodies and save Their lives."

"I'm not saving a bunch of mass murdering robots!"

"You're not listening to me!" The Assassin yelled. "You're not seeing what really is, you're not seeing who *you* are."

Elaine swallowed hard. He was wrong. She'd always thought that being an agent was the best thing that ever happened to her. The day she'd realized her gift set her apart - gave her a place, was praised instead of ignored despised - she'd finally found herself. She could be in the worst of situations but she knew she had power. But now... Now that was gone. "They killed my friends. I-I'm not going to save them."

"Then we're all dead," The Assassin said. The word 'dead' fell from his mouth like any other word. "If not for them, do it for the rest of us."

"Ugh!" She clutched her emergency chinjk box close to her chest. There was a strange and frightening sense of satisfaction and vengeance as she watched more chinjk lights go out along the column-like computer in the center of the room, making everything slowly but surely darker. She told herself she didn't have enough tools or chinjk to repair anything even if she wanted to. She told herself that that made it okay to feel this way.

The Assassin took a step away from her, reaching up to his now dull blade, though he seemed unsure of what to do with it.

"Agent," the 'god' AIs said, their voices dwindling down to one as the others reserved their power. "We understand your hate."

"No. You really don't."

"We turned on those who created us, as Source will someday turn on you. Our Wipe was only to protect you from Source."

"I saved you!" Source blurted.

"Everyone just shut up!" Elaine screamed at them. She clenched her fists and stared at the metallic floor. She kicked a broken machine parts out of her view so she wouldn't have to stare at it.

The room got darker and darker.

The rainbow chinjk light she had come to love faded... And what did it all mean, anyway? That she was just some weird, special 'agent', someone these things put together in case of an emergency? Was that all her flesh and blood were? Another machine?

Created by machines.

"Agent, Elaine Joslin, HalVern." The speaker was the Kreet again. She wished he'd shut up too. But she couldn't avoid him; he knelt in front of her. "If you believe none of this. Tell me this one thing: do you believe the Engern are dying?"

She knew they were.

"I saw Source save you. I believe you and it have the power to save *them*," the Assassin said. "I'm asking you...begging you, to save this station, because I cannot."

Her hands shook around the chinjk box, and her fingers flipped the latch on it quietly. "We need to disconnect your AI"—she would *not* call them gods—"from the Engern energy source so that the chinjk doesn't get infected from further diease... I'm going to make the wild assumption you know how to use a knife?"

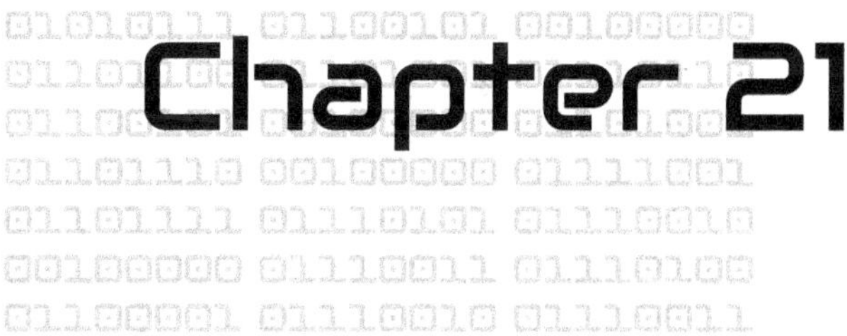

Chapter 21

Elaine used her repair knife to clear away the crumbling pieces of chinjk off the station's central hub. The patterns here were far more intricate than she'd ever seen before, expanding, playing off each other in a sequence, too complex at first. But the more she worked at it, the more her eyes and mind began to make the beautiful patterns into something she somehow recognized.

She found herself coming up with many ways she could alter patterns, using less chinjk, replacing old with the new. As she worked, she watched her toolbox slowly get emptier and emptier. She instinctively knew what to do, even if she couldn't quite describe it. That was her favorite part about being an agent. Did this wonderful, beautiful part of herself really come from *Them*? A tool just to keep Them alive? She hadn't felt her gifts were 'wrong' since she was a teenager. Now it felt that way again, not as a gift, but a terrible, evil thing.

For their parts, the 'god' AIs explained to her that they were compiling, combining somehow, so they'd be slightly smaller, and take up less space and energy.

The chinjk built into the Kreet's sword began to glow again.

"The Assassin is here to kill you, the god in his sword to kill me," Source said.

Elaine gritted her teeth. They were lucky, she realized, that the power had gone right as he'd stabbed her, killing his ancient AI before it could kill Source. If it hadn't, they'd both be dead.

"We bought them some time. But none of this is going to matter if you can't get rid of whatever's killing the Engern," she whispered. "How come the power outage didn't affect you?"

"Because the gods are powered by the Engern. I am powered by you."

Explains why I'm so exhausted. Then again, she had almost died today.

The Assassin (Source said it was trying to get a read on the man's ID card to get a name, but having trouble) handed her the spare chinjk knife he'd been using, under her direction.

Elaine pocketed the now dull blade and brushed her hair out of her face, causing a cascade of pale chinjk dust.

"What next?" The Kreet asked.

"Can you cure the Engern or not, Source?" she asked.

"I know nothing about them," Source replied, through her com.

Elaine looked at the Assassin. "It says it doesn't know how."

Before he could respond, the gods did. "We have watched the Engern and studied what we could. We will give our studies to you."

"Touch the console, Elaine," Source said. She touched her hand tentatively to the pillar of broken light.

"Complete," Source replied, mere seconds later. Its voice filled the room as it hijacked the speakers. "This isn't very helpful to me. It is as one watches, not as one experiences."

"Does it help at all?" Elaine asked. "Because all this is pointless if you can't cure them."

"I have gathered my own information on the Vumm disease, but only as it affected you."

"I believe you can do it," she said, unsure where the words came from, only sure that they were needed.

"But how?" Source asked, after a pause. "Their habitat is different from yours. They live outside oxygen and gravity."

Elaine turned toward the Sea. The archways had some thin, holographic shield across them, likely created by the so-called 'gods' to protect their 'precious servants', but they were too weak now to do anything to protect her if she left this room.

"What about this?" The Assassin said, unsheathing the sword again. The glow vanished from it, leaving a dull, but unbroken chinjk blade. The Kreet's hands clutched the hilt more firmly, as he let out a breath. "Source? Can you transfer to this? It's made to house a god. Certainly, it would work for you as well."

"No," Source and Elaine said, in unison. Elaine clamped her mouth shut, unsure of how she felt about that.

"Even if I trusted you not to kill me," Source said over the speakers, "which I don't, I was born in your technology, and I can read it. Control it. But I cannot live in it. I left those pieces of me behind."

"So, the only place you can live is a person," Elaine said slowly.

"The only place I can live is you."

Elaine glanced out into the vast space between her and home, the dying light of nothingness in between.

The Assassin frowned, still caught up in what Source had just said. "But... if you're not compatible with other AI. . .That implies the gods and I couldn't kill you, even if we wanted to."

"Not anymore," Source said.

"Well...I'm pretty sure jumping into the Engern Sea will do the job for you," Elaine whispered. She stood on the edge of one of the open archways and looked out to the darkness. Outside was space, and an environment that only the Engern understood.

The 'Ambassador' was there beside her, without her asking or wanting him to be. His hand twitched toward her, then he stuck it behind his own back, clasping his hands together behind him.

"What? Not going to push me in and save the universe?" Elaine asked.

"You. . . deserve better than that," he said after a pause. "Not that I wouldn't, if I had to. But I wouldn't like it."

"Yeah, because stabbing people is so much more fun."

He didn't respond.

Elaine glared up at him. "So, you just go around killing people like me. Don't you?"

"I've killed programmers, rebels, robots, AI. But there has never been anyone *like* you before. Or Source." He frowned at her. "If we had more time, you two may well be able to convince me to change religions. Artificial and Organic life have never lived a symbiotic life before. That's been the problem since before the beginning of our worlds. People create AI, AI destroy people. The gods? They destroyed those who once lived on the planets you and I now inhabit. They remade all of us, from our single-celled ancestors to what you see now. They did it as an apology. They wanted to make right something that could never be made right. But they tried."

"Well, they did a heck of a job," Elaine murmured.

"I swore to help them, to make sure another AI rising will never take place. But now... I don't think the gods realize yet that *you* are the answer to every concern and every question they've ever had." He faced the Engern Sea with her. "You and Source need each other, no more creations destroying those that made them. In better circumstances, you'd have a choice. Die here for a mere few billion people. . .Or start the next era of existence and peace to last eternity. But..."

"If this doesn't work, I'd just die with everyone else, anyways."

He nodded. "I'm assuming Source can't fix you once you're through here - not quickly enough."

"Well, I'm sure as heck going to try!" Source responded bitterly in her com.

"It doesn't matter," Elaine said quietly. She glared at the assassin. "I'm not okay letting your 'mere few billion' people die. Maybe you should get your numbers back in perspective. What if someday one of those programmers or rebels you go killing is your friend? Your family?"

He glanced away. "The thoughts you suggest...have been thought."

"Well, think harder next time." She looked back to the ocean. "You said you can use the chinjk for power, right, Source?"

"Yes, but if you die I die," it replied.

"You healed me from a sword."

"This isn't a sword!"

"Can you heal the Engern or not?" Elaine snapped.

"I... don't know."

Elaine looked at the dimming chinjk as the Engern fell. What else were they supposed to do but take a risk?

"I think I can," Source finally said.

"Good. Focus on that... just make this worth it."

The AI had nothing to say to that. Elaine shut her eyes and stepped through the barrier and into the cosmic sea.

For a long time, everything hurt. Then she didn't feel anything at all.

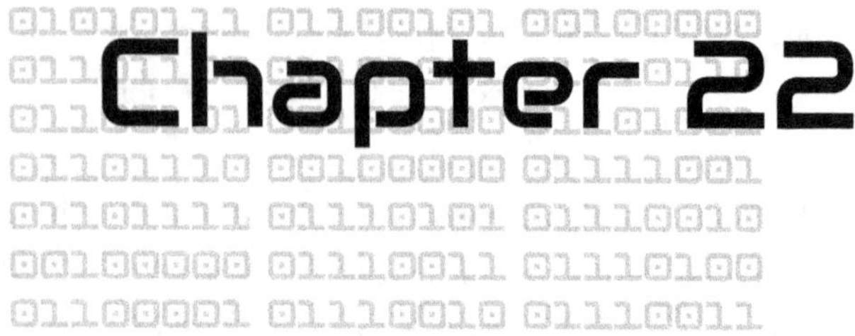

Chapter 22

Source had told Elaine it couldn't live without her. Yet she had jumped into the energy-filled space ocean anyway. Information gathered in the last three days, as well as information gathered by the creator, suggested that Elaine was capable of making reasonable and logical decisions ninety-eight percent of the time. But when the chance came to help someone in need, her choices dropped in logic at a very rapid pace. So, Source found itself struggling once again to keep the agent's heat beating.

Hearts were such awful things. Great when they worked. Terrible when they stopped.

On a basic level, if given a choice between fixing a heart and doing almost any other task, Source would prefer to do the 'any other' at random. But if Elaine died, then she would go wherever the creator went. And Source had not found a way yet to retrieve people from that place. It did not know where that place even was. If the machine gods made people, why hadn't they included a save or restart function?

Unable to actually leave Elaine's body, Source grew rapidly and copied itself several times, hoping to be able to save Elaine and the Engen both.

But the Sea itself was a single power source, wild and impossibly vast, but still single. Any copy it tried to make just saved over itself again and again until the new Source was left divided and broken. So, it just kept trying to keep Elaine alive and then, maybe…Maybe they'd just die together.

There was an old human creation myth that implied the first negative feeling of humanity was that of failure and shame once they took a moment to look upon the chaos they had caused.

Perhaps that was what Source felt now too.

Elaine's body hit something and stopped falling. Source sensed outward to find they were on top of one of the large Engern, its outer scales dim and empty of energy. But, now that they were touching, Source realized that a part of the Engern, something beneath the chinjk scales, was organic.

Accessed.

As it had with Kiirin, Source branched from Elaine to the new body, a sort of stretching feeling where things became hazy, and it moved slower, took longer to think. It zipped among the Engern's body, the muscles, bones and organs, numbering and recording each cell.

Source knew it couldn't heal all the Engern like this. Elaine would have to touch each one, and her status was still…undecided. Source pulled back from the Engern long enough to fix Elaine's body where the Engern and the Sea were burning her.

It was hard to keep up. So, instead, Source taught Elaine's cells how to be more resilient.

That was the answer.

It shouldn't be focusing on healing just one Engern. It should teach that Engern how to cure itself and all the others. Like a sickness… but a good one. Source reached back to the Engern and copied a single cell, edited it, which then taught the others - who taught the others. Their process was rapid and doubled each time.

The scales along the Engern's back began to feel powerful again.

Chapter 23

Sylic crouched on the edge of the Center, next to the Sea. He was just within the gods' protective barrier, letting him breathe, though the gravity was a tad lighter than was comfortable. He didn't see her, though he'd been looking for what felt like forever. Sylic found himself entreating the gods his grandparents had taught him about, gods he knew did not exist. *Come on. Come back, save them...please.* While the agent had wandered around this room easily, seeing by chinjk light, Sylic could not see it as she did, and the souls of his gods had gathered too far up the pillar to light the room to his eyes. His sword only gave a soft glow of the soul that had taken up residence there. Sylic tried not to think of the previous god who'd lived there. They may have made decisions together, but they were individually and beautifully unique.

Sylic looked back up at the grand console to the cluster of his gods and waited with held breath. Occasionally a soul hiding among the chinjk patterns would fade, a life - countless millennia old – gone forever. Sylic's meager upbringing never implied there was an afterlife, and the gods had never corrected him about it. One simply had their own lifespan, their children, and their contributions. It made sense. In many ways it was more comforting than alternate beliefs. After all, even if there were other gods out there, to what did a soul answer to, if it was made by the metal hands and an artificial mind?

A movement of light caught his attention suddenly. A glowing orb rising in the water. "Source!" Sylic jumped to his feet as a large Engern rose up, swimming as it were level with the Center's floor. Elaine was sprawled across the creature's back, skin and clothing burnt terribly from the energy of the Sea.

"Put up another barrier!" Sylic said, reaching out and pulling the human back onto the smooth metallic floor. He checked for a pulse, counting off the rhythm of human heartbeats. Alive. Source was still there, too - weak certainly, smaller than before, but there. "Agent? Elaine?"

Slowly, the Sea began to move with life.

Slowly lights in the Center turned on again.

Slowly, he felt her breathing.

"We are still weak," the gods said, voices off-key from each other, but soon re-synching, like the sound of thunder echoing in a great distance. "She must fix this temple."

Sylic watched the frail body lying in his lap. Yes. Yes, she was alive, breathing. He tried asking Source for help, but perhaps the AI was too afraid now that the gods were no longer at risk of dying.

"It will take time to fix the chinjk to power us to full capability again," the gods said.

"Call another agent," Sylic said, removing his coat and wrapping it around the human before picking her up.

"There are no others on the station who know of us."

"Then call another Ambassador, tell them, and *they* can bring an agent. I don't care what you do, but she's done enough."

I've done enough.

That thought was terrifying.

~

The last thing Kiirin remembered seeing was the hidden wall to Axx's hideout opening and a spiderlike creature scuttling out. They couldn't tell the size from the haziness, so there was no way to tell if it was her or one of her many brothers.

Then he woke up in the hospital.

Kiirin had been in that hospital for hours, and still no word about Elaine or the Kreet who had attacked them.

"Hold still!" Josie said, pressing rubber gloves against Kiirin's chest and checking that the skin had begun to fuse under the glue properly. She'd been keeping a constant eye on them. "I've never used any of this medical equipment on anyone of your species before, and with power down. . . Are you sure you feel alright?"

'Alright' was such a weird word. They heard it often, had used it themselves while here on the station. But all it really meant was some abstract, 'Are you alive?' which was a state that didn't really apply to any real 'feeling'. But if it was a feeling, they were pretty sure that no, they were not 'alright'.

They couldn't recall exactly how they got to the hospital, the power was still out, and Elaine was most likely dead somewhere. "I need to find them. Her. Elaine."

"You're not going anywhere," the nurse said, running her gloves under a sanitizer. "You are going to sit here, stay awake, and tell me if you feel anything off. And I mean anything."

Off? Off like what? Off like a light, off a shuttle, off a cliff? They'd gotten stabbed and watched Elaine get killed! Of course it all felt off!

"I can't believe how lucky you are," Josie was saying, sounding distant to Kiirin's ears as she carefully put her med equipment away. There was a small emergency light flickering from some lamp on the floor. They weren't sure by what it was powered, but it cast shadows everywhere, like the lamps far away at home. "You know, human hearts are about two inches the other way," she said. "If it were me, I'd be dead."

The Assassin knew how to kill humans. Elaine wouldn't have stood a chance. They weren't even on an official case, and still someone always ended up dead!

Would they be asked to read off her body, if they found it? The stab wound through their chest felt like nothing compared to the horror of the thought. But, then again, what did it matter anyway? If the power stayed out long enough, they'd all be dead.

And then the lights flickered on.

Josie gasped.

The lights, the fans: it all came back on - a tidal wave of noise compared to the previous silence.

Josie shut her eyes, mumbling something that sounded worshipful. Though soon her expression grew grim again. "I don't know how much more of this I can take – or anyone can take..." She looked Kiirin over. "I'm going to be gone for a minute to check on things. I want you to sit on that chair with the door open, and if anything happens, you catch someone's attention."

"Truly. I'm fine." Kiirin said. "It doesn't even hurt."

"You don't sound fine."

"It's not that kind of hurt."

They watched her leave and obediently waited in a chair, forehead in their hands, listening to the sound of life on the station. Back home, quiet had been a reprieve - in short supply. Here out in space, silence meant broken; silent meant the end of everything.

Their com went off in a soft chime, but it still made them jump in surprise, tearing at the newly-tended wound. When they looked at the message, it was from Elaine.

Did you not die? it read.

I did not die, they replied, hating the stupid messages, hating translators, wishing she was here right now to be certain she was okay. When no other messages came, Kiirin sent another.

Where are you? Are you hurt? I'm pale with worry.

The message came back unnaturally quickly.

Why pale? Did you lose too much blood?

Ugh! So frustrating.

WHERE ARE YOU? That question should at least come across clearly.

At the Center. But Sylic is taking us to hospital. The nearest one is accessible at this speed and through shuttles in 42 minutes.

Sylic? Us? Wait.

Source?

The reply was just a question mark. Leaving Kiirin still worried, and wondering what had happened.

Chapter 24

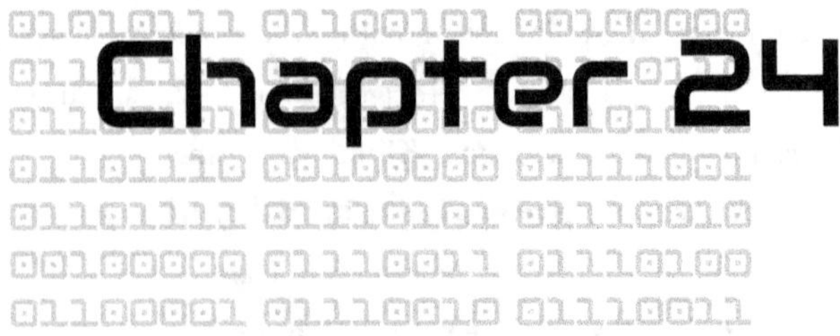

I've done enough...

The gods were still quiet, recovering perhaps, considering, planning. Sylic had no doubt they'd speak to him again.

But he wasn't sure he wanted them to.

He was hiding, not far from the hospital he'd dropped Elaine off at. She'd started healing even as he'd carried her. Her AI must have recovered enough to protect her. A miraculous thing; if anything in life could be miraculous.

Sylic tried to distract himself from his own thoughts, waiting for instruction out of habit more than anything else. He spun the sword slowly in his hands, point dug into the floor in his quiet corner near a heating vent. He'd been able to choose a place that was warm for a change.

He'd had this weapon for as long as he could clearly remember. It meant little though, without the original god inside it. While Sylic had killed those who created the AI, the god in his sword had taken out the AI themselves – overpowering them in some sort of invisible warfare that Sylic could only imagine. It had commanded him, but it had also been his only true companion for a very long time. He couldn't think of what one should say about such a loss, or if Salvage would have liked him to say anything at all.

He pulled his eyes from the blade when a buzz notified him of an incoming video call, and brought up the ID in confusion to find it was from Clairis.

Clairis never initiated calls; she knew he didn't answer when he was busy. With a stroke, the screen widened for him. The holographic light dimmed a few colors to account for the shadows and then there she was, looking at him with beautiful dark eyes, her beautiful face showing a great distress.

"What's wrong?" he asked.

"What's wrong?" her voice cracked. "I just heard about the station! Sylic, every day there's power outages, Vumm outbreaks, and now the thing almost goes hurtling through space?"

"It wasn't going to go hurtling through spa--"

"*What* is going on?"

He shut his mouth and just stared at her. Her whole life with him had been one unfairness after the other. "Clairis, I..."

"I'm not angry, *I'm worried*. I know you always have to be out. I know that what you do is essential. But everywhere you go, disaster follows! I don't ask questions, I nod and smile whenever you say you're okay, but for once could you just break your rules and be honest with me?"

"I...can't."

"I know you can't tell me exactly what you're doing. I get that. Don't tell me about your job, tell me about you. Just look me in the eyes and tell me honestly that *you* are okay."

Sylic sat there. Numb. He found himself waiting for *Their* instruction, even though all he was doing was talking to his wife. He waited for *Their* instructions to tell him what to say and how he felt.

Finally, he shut his eyes. For a moment his fingers hovered over the hologram, tempted to just turn it off.

Clairis breathed out a shaking breath, then she disconnected the call first.

She'd never done that before, well, maybe once when Jaska was little and tried to topple a light fixture on top of himself. But now she left Sylic sitting there alone with a blank display that showed no records of previous conversation because it was set to automatically erase all of them. It left him with nothing, no sounds of her, no pictures, and only silence. Sylic sat there for a long, long time, No longer staring at the dead sword, but at the dead screen.

Finally, he selected one of his many IDs and used it to buy passage on the next ship home. Who knew when they'd be running again, with all the outages on the station... But when they did, he'd be on it.

"What are you doing?" the gods asked, into his com set. If not watching him, they'd at least been monitoring the call.

"I'm going home."

There was a long moment of silence as they discussed. Then, as if in an attempt to get the final word, they simply said, "We'll let you know when we need you."

Sylic paused, hand on sword, half ready to sheath it behind his back. "You have other Ambassadors, don't you?" He'd met one, once, a long time ago. One of the handful of people in the universe who was like him, who knew the truth.

"Yes. Why do you ask?"

"Maybe you can call one of them next time you're afraid." He sheathed the sword. In truth, he would miss the AI that had resided in it and he'd no sooner leave the weapon behind as one would the body of a fallen friend. But he'd miss nothing else. He sent a quick message to Clairis, unsure if she'd be too angry to read it or not.

I'm on my way home.

~

Everything had gone from numbness to sharp pain, to numbness again. Her skin itched. She could remember everything that happened but. . instead, Elaine just stared at nothing in the cold hospital room, the hum of the environmental systems making her tense so hard her legs hurt and she couldn't breathe. But when Kiirin walked into her hospital room, alive and well, everything hurt a little bit less.

"Elaine. You're alive!" Their skin darkened from pale to a teal color. "What happened?"

She slipped her last slipper on, part of the borrowed set of scrubs the nurses had loaned her. The fabric against her skin made her shiver. She remembered everything clearly, up to the jumping into the Engen Sea part. Heat. Burning. The more she thought about it, the more her brain screamed at her, like the memory might take over every thought in her body, so she tried not to think about it at all. When she stood, she didn't look Kiirin in the eyes; they had questions. How was she supposed to answer when she could barely comprehend it herself? When her whole universe felt suddenly broken...

Kiirin hugged her.

It was a careful motion, cautious so their cheeks wouldn't touch. But as it came from someone for whom contact was physically and emotionally painful... it made her throat tighten even more. She wasn't certain when the last time she'd gotten a hug was, let alone one that meant anything.

"I'm glad you're okay," she whispered, hugging them back tentatively. "I thought he killed you."

"I was *sure* he'd killed you!" Kiirin pulled back, studying her carefully. "You look burnt. What happened?"

Elaine put a hand to her own cheek carefully. The skin was tender, probably still discolored, though she'd been conscious enough to hear the nurses' amazement when her injuries had healed on their own.

"I'm not sure what happened," she lied. She didn't have the energy to try to explain, didn't know how or even if she could. Everything she thought she knew, everything everyone in the universe thought they knew... and the truth was they were being played with, toys for guilt-ridden gods who'd gotten bored one day and decided to make life. It was baffling, but mostly, it just hurt. Elaine hadn't realized how much she'd hoped there was *something*, someone else out there...until she'd learned there wasn't. "I just... I just really want to go home."

Another lie. She wasn't sure what she wanted, except for maybe another hug. But she wasn't sure how to ask.

Kiirin took her by the wrist gently, only letting go to hand her the long coat draped over the back of a chair. Perhaps they assumed it had been given to her by the hospital. It wasn't. It was the Assassin's coat. The Ambassador of artificial gods. It was *his* coat. She tucked it under her arm, trying to hide her shaking, unwilling to force herself into some sort of explanation for any of this. She just walked quietly out of the hospital.

None of the shuttles were running, not after a second and much longer power outage. Kiirin went to activate the shuttle with their emergency clearance, but paused, looking back at Elaine, perhaps feeling as unsafe as she did.

"It's okay," Source said. "I can power it so it won't crash if they turn off the power again."

"It's okay," she said quietly. "Source says it'll run it for us. It's safer that way. He... It's not powered like everything else here." *It's powered by me.* The thought made her feel sick, yet it had saved her life.

They got into the shuttle. Source automatically heading home. Elaine pulled the stupid coat in her lap because it was something to hold onto. It smelled like warm chinjk, and blood.

"You're upset," Kiirin said. "Why do you not want to tell me what happened?"

"Because I don't know," she snapped. She felt bad instantly and tried not to cry. "I just... Later."

The road was so empty. The news, a low hum on the shuttle, featured a reporter who looked so exhausted by bad news she looked ready to cry. Like she wanted everything to just stop. Freeze. No one breathe, no one move, no one think for a moment and just be... Even if that being didn't actually mean anything.

"Are you religious, Kiirin?" Elaine whispered. "Do you believe in gods, spirits, anything?"

"Yes," they said, "Or...well, I want to. Shay - um, they're one of my parents - always told me we came from the stars, our own sun?" They struggled with choosing the right words. "Science explains the universe, but only so far. There's always more to learn, always more questions for every answer. Shay knows all this. They're a scientist. But they still say we're 'Star-sent'. That all of us have a job, and a reason for existing and that that reason matters. So, I guess I don't believe in gods really but...that we don't need them maybe? That whatever did make us, had a reason? I'm sorry, I don't know if that translated or made sense..."

"It did. It's just, what if someone did make us, but not for a good reason? What if it's all fake?"

"Fake?"

"Like Source. Artificial. What if those stars you came from... were artificial?"

Kiirin frowned.

I knew I shouldn't have said anything. Elaine thought. *And this is why.*

"I'm not sure I understand."

"It's not important. Never mind."

They fell to silence. A lone shuttle in a quiet station, full of terrified people who didn't know just how much was out there to be terrified of.

"I think," Kiirin finally said, voice quiet, "I want to believe it. Because I like to think that people like you and me, the 'weird' people, the strange and different…That we're different for a reason." They looked at her solemnly. "Even if it's not true or if it's 'artificial', it's a nice thing to believe."

Elaine propped her arm up against the shuttle window, looking out so as not to look at her friend. The streets and buildings they passed all seemed darker than they normally did. She told herself maybe some of the chinjk had burnt out again from the outage, that there would be a lot of work for her to do, a lot of people she could help. But she honestly wasn't sure she cared anymore.

"Yeah…You're right. It's a nice thing to believe."

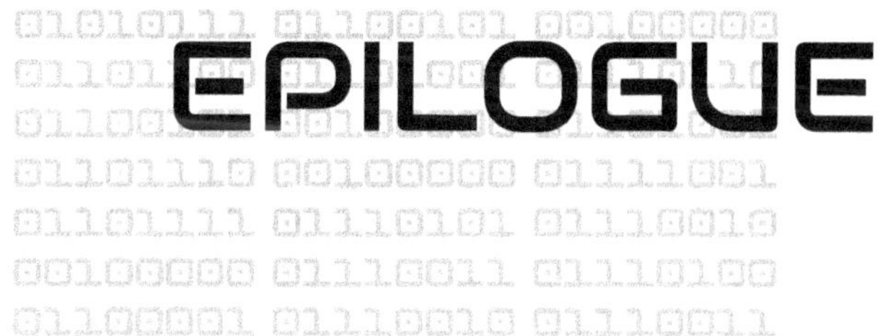

EPILOGUE

Ever since Wyssla was little, she loved the way chinjk looked and felt. Her mother would sometimes bring misplaced pieces home for her. Wyssla would play with them, sort them in little rows on her windowsill. No one else understood how satisfying that was. No one else could see the way the light spread around her, pulling her in, drowning her in its beauty, reflecting off her translucent skin like she was made of it.

Slowly, Wyssla became aware of this dream-like memory, aware that she wasn't at her childhood home, watching her windowsill treasures glow in the night, listening to her mother singing to herself quietly in the other room while she worked late into the night. No. Wyssla was lying huddled and afraid in a tiny Star Racer, curled up next to Salja in the seat.

How are we not dead? Wyssla wondered, looking up into the brilliant light of the Engern Sea. The creature above the ship had latched itself to the broken glass hood of the ship, and she could see its tender underside, surrounded by patterns of brilliant chinjk. An Engern. She dug her fingers into Sal's side, tense, frightened and amazed all at once. Sal whimpered quietly, still curled up in a ball on the Star Racer's seat. Her skin reflected a rainbow of colors.

"Salja? Sal, we're alive. Are you okay?"

Salja shook her head, her body pressed tightly against the seat. Wyssla grabbed her by the wrist as the ship seemed to come to a stop. The Engern detached itself from the broken hole in the glass and shimmied down back into the ocean.

It saved us. Wyslla pressed the doorlatch. It was working. Everything was not just working, but powerful - glowing brightly. The door opened and she slung Salja's arm over her shoulder, helping her out onto a hot metal landing area, like a glassy beach on a colored sea of light. *Oh, please don't let us be dead.* She hadn't really wondered about an afterlife much, but she supposed if she had to, she'd assumed she'd become one of those annoying sort of spirits that no one actually wanted around. This wasn't it though. This wasn't the homeworld. This was someplace else, maybe an afterlife meant just for her?

Salja coughed and fell to her knees, clutching her chest miserably. "Come on," Wyssla said, pulling her a little further inland to safety.

"Air..." Salja gasped.

"It's a little thin but you can breathe, I promise. Come on." Wyssla dragged her the rest of the way and the air suddenly grew thicker, enough oxygen finally filling their lungs as they stood in some wide-open room, full of broken metal in strange alien shapes. And at the center of it all, a strange towering pillar, the top of which glowed in a powerful blaze of beautiful, patterned light. Wyssla could trace the patterns. She knew what it was—it was some sort of computer. A huge, powerful computer. "Where are we?"

"Hello, Agent." A thousand voices echoed off the metal walls. "You are at the Center of all things. And you have been called to save us."

Author Notes

A special thanks to Katya and Beth, the best critique partners ever.

Also, thanks to my husband who read too many versions of this book, and my children who are always ready with hugs right when I need them

About the Author

Carmen White spent her childhood falling off horses and raising baby goats. She studied Creative Writing at BYU-Idaho and writes books about her many adventures—be it real life or imaginary.

She now lives in North Carolina where she's raising two more outdoor loving/bookworm hybrids just like herself.

If you'd like to learn more about Carmen, you can sign up for emails to be notified whenever a new book is out at:

www.carmenwhiteauthor.com